Vandana Singh

"Sweeping starscapes and daring cosmology . . . make Singh a worthy heir to Cordwainer Smith and Arthur C. Clarke."
—Chris Moriarty, *Fantasy & Science Fiction*

"Vandana Singh's science fiction . . . highlights the interplay between scientific and mythic narratives, focusing on the ways that 'stories make the world.' She combines seemingly opposed categories, such as tradition and modernity, human and animal (or machine), the urban and the natural, and—most frequently—myth and science."
—Michael Saler, *Times Literary Supplement*

"There's a wonderful discordance between the cool, reflective quality of Singh's prose and the colorful imagery and powerful longing in her narratives."
—*Washington Post*

D0191107

Utopias of the Third Kind

plus

PM PRESS OUTSPOKEN AUTHORS SERIES

PM PRESS OUTSPOKEN AUTHORS SERIES

Utopias of the Third Kind

plus

Lamentations in a Lost Tongue

plus

Arctic Sky

and much more

Vandana Singh

PM PRESS | 2022

"Lamentations in a Lost Tongue," original to this volume, is a selection from
    a yet unfinished longer story.
"Arctic Sky" was first published in *Eat the Sky, Drink the Ocean*, Zubaan
    Books, 2014.
"Utopias of the Third Kind" is original to this volume.
"Hunger" was first published in *Interfictions: An Anthology of Interstitial
    Writing*, Small Beer Press, 2007.
"The Room on the Roof" was first published in *Polyphony*, Wheatland Press,
    2002.
"True Journey Is Return: A Tribute to Ursula K. Le Guin" was published in
    Antariksh Yatra, Vandana Singh's blog, 2018.

ISBN (paperback): 9781629639154
ISBN (ebook): 9781629639246
LCCN: 2021936608

Series editor: Terry Bisson
Cover design by John Yates/www.stealworks.com
Author photo by Claudia Ruiz Gustafson
Insides by Jonathan Rowland

10 9 8 7 6 5 4 3 2 1

Printed in the USA

Contents

Lamentations in a Lost Tongue

I MET HIM IN a town in California. I had been wandering aimlessly, looking into shop windows, and found myself before an optician's. I was looking unseeingly at a tower of artificial tears in the window of the store, thinking about what to do next, and plagued by a faint sense of melancholy. Then the reflection of a man appeared next to my own and I turned to find beside me a thin, spare, older man about my height. He was dressed in a long-sleeved shirt and corduroy pants, and he was dark brown, with a fine, lined, handsome face. His black hair was streaked with gray. There was a subtle sense of his being out of place—in a very different way than the displaced feeling that was my own constant companion. He was staring at the display of artificial tears.

"Do you know what that is?" he asked, looking at me for the first time.

"Artificial tears?" I said, puzzled.

"*Asombroso*," he said softly, staring at the display. Then, louder, looking at me:

"Amazing! So much sorrow in the whole wide world that we have run out of tears and they must make more!"

He gave a short laugh that was half wonder, half something else I couldn't name, smiled politely at me, and turned and walked down the street. As he walked away I saw the burden of a heavy sorrow on his stooped shoulders; yet he walked with energy, with a spring in his step.

Urged by a sudden compulsion, I hurried after him.

"Please, I'd like to speak with you." I looked around a little wildly, and there, like a miracle, was a café with outdoor tables. "A cup of coffee?"

With the coffee before us, I tried to engage him in conversation. Between his fair English and my schoolgirl Spanish, we managed quite well. I had thought he was, perhaps, from the highlands of Mexico, somewhere remote. It turned out he was an insurance agent in a small town in Peru. He had grown up in a village up the mountain from the town, where his family had farmed with increasing difficulty, as the mountain springs dried up. His ancestry was mixed Spanish and Indigenous, he said. He was a widower, visiting his daughter and her family, his first trip away from the small town. He spoke of the awe he had felt arriving in Lima. And then to take a plane, to fly above the mountains, over the clouds to LA! It had been profoundly disorienting.

"I've seen it on TV," he said. "I know the world is full of marvels. But to walk in these streets—that's something else."

"Do you ever go back to your village?" I asked him.

"Not often," he said. A distant look came into his eyes—he saw, not the clamor of the street before us, but the high mountains of the village. I felt him slipping away from our conversation. I wanted to hold on to him, to tell him—look, in some way I don't understand, we're related. Not by blood but something more subtle. And I wanted to know the nature of the great sorrow he carried. It seemed to me that the shadows around him carried the weight and tears of something larger than one person's life. Fanciful thought! But that urgency compelled me to pull out the sketch of what I called *the symbol* and push it across the table to him.

"I'm wondering," I said, as I had so many times before, "whether you've seen anything like this before."

He came back from wherever he was and stared at the piece of paper. He started to shake his head. Then he stared at it again. Abruptly, his shoulders sagged. He covered his face with his hands. He looked at me.

"I have never seen such a thing," he said. "But—it reminds me. There's a place up over my village, where the spring was. The water used to come out from under a rock and circle down, something like this, this *espiral* . . . Spiral? Yes. And when you looked up from one place where I liked to sit, you would see the sun in the center of the two peaks. Of the mountain. Like in your picture, but it is not quite the same. Enough to remind me."

People have said different things about the symbol. To one person, it's a woman, arms flung out, dancing; they ignore the broken spiral. To another person the spiral reminds them of something they've seen, perhaps a pattern on a carpet, but the dot and the wings or arms are a peripheral add-on. This man was among the few to whom the symbol meant something in its entirety.

The symbol is my excuse for the aimless wanderings of my early retirement. Since there is no particular direction, no rudder in my life, I have clung to this fortuitous discovery, a rough sketch on a crumpled piece of paper that I found in a park in Delhi. Not having any compelling stories of my own in a life of unrelenting ordinariness, I have found that *the symbol* gives me access, for a while, to the far more interesting lives of others. Stories in which I become, for a brief moment, a listener or receiver, if not a participant. After all, every word written needs a blank page, every song a silence against which the notes are heard.

"Please, do tell me, more," I said. I saw the tears rise in his dark eyes.

"The spring," he said. "The first thing I remember seeing as a child. It was life to our village. My mother—she used to send us children to the high pool to get the water, in the summers when the big one dried out."

Through his words I saw the arid, rocky rise of the mountainside, the streaks of snow on the high slopes like banners. The wind blowing cold and dry. The patient llamas on an outcrop against the sky. The father, face weathered by the sun and toil, in a stony field of alfalfa. The high, clear voices of children, and against it all, the constant, reassuring sound of water, faint but discernible. The boy standing at the very spot where, at a certain time in the afternoon, the sun would be exactly between two peaks on the top of the mountain, and you could see the glacial meltwater meandering down the slope, circling around the outcrops, to fall into a pool as cold and clear as the winter sky. From here it overflowed into a thin stream that fed a larger pool near the village below. One evening the boy's uncle came from a town two valleys away to visit, saying he could take his nephew back with him, to school and a job and a new life.

The boy had come to this spot to think. He saw the sun above the mountain, and the water. And then the water turned into a mighty stream and came roaring down, but when it got to him it vanished, and there was, just as suddenly, nothing—just dry desert and the sun beating down, and the sense of terrible loss. At this point the boy sank to his knees in horror, but suddenly he was back in the normal world, with the water spiraling down as before and the tips of his dusty old shoes wet with it.

"I had seen a vision," he told me. "It said the spring would flood, and then dry up, and there would be no more farming. But I didn't know that then. I told my parents what I had seen, and they looked at each other, and they let me go. I left my village and became—someone else. My parents refused to leave, so I would go to see them and my sisters and brothers. Three years before they died, there was a flood, and my youngest brother was one of the ones killed. The next summer the stream dried up."

I sensed that was not the end of the story. He took a sip of his coffee, grimaced, and bit into the pastry. He passed his hand over his eyes.

"Wherever I go" he said. He stopped, cleared his throat. I felt again the presence of a sorrow much larger than the man before me.

"Wherever I go," he said, "I get a feeling. Not the vision, that's only happened one other time."

He didn't tell me about the other time. He said that whenever he is close to water, or where water might have been, he senses its past or future. He knows, for example, that there's the ghost of a waterfall in the rocky mountainside behind the row of shops. No trace remains that is obvious to the eye, but it is there, and he can tell that the water is cascading down and through the shoe store, and over the street, splashing us as it goes past. No matter where he goes, he is haunted by the ghosts of streams, rivers, and pools. His one trip to the ocean was so overwhelming that he cannot even talk about it. So he stays in his small town, where he knows his ghosts, and he visits the sacred pools and springs as a man might visit friends who will understand his craziness, and because they give him some peace.

"I came all the way here," he said, smiling a little, "because my daughter insisted. I had to come. I was afraid, but now I am here. Thank you for the coffee, and for listening. You are very kind."

I didn't stop him when, after a while, he got up to leave. I resisted the urge to tell him I would like to know him better, that I felt a connection between us that must mean something. We said our goodbyes, and I watched him walk along the street. He didn't need any artificial tears. I understood at last what kinds of sorrows he carried with him as he left the sidewalk to walk along the curving edge of the vanished stream.

It was then that it came to me that the land itself is a page on which a greater and more complex story is continually being written—that what I called "the symbol" was perhaps a fragment, a letter of that script which only a few have learned to read. That we carry around with us, perhaps consciously, perhaps not, ghostly sorrows that may well be dirges, laments in ancient, earthy languages long forgotten.

Because a story needs its silences, I will not tell you whether I met him again the next day. I will not tell you whether we talked until dawn in an outdoor café, whether he and I went tracing the vanished streams of that town for the entire week that I was there, whether I got to know him in the dark of my hotel room with the fireflies dancing against the window, whether, after the sweet comfort that strangers who are not strangers can give to each other after lifetimes of being apart, I have begun to hear, very faintly, the sound of rushing water underneath the asphalt and concrete veneer of civilization, a song in a language I hope someday to understand.

Arctic Sky

I was let out of prison on my seventeenth birthday. That was yesterday.

*

Eight months ago I was a different person. Everything was different. There was, for instance, the light of sun on snow, the endless sea, the sky of the Arctic. I thought I was brave, a rebel taking on the greatest cause in the history of humankind. On the ship *Valiant*, sailing from Northern Canada to the East Siberian Sea, the light reminded me of a certain look I remembered in my mother's eyes. Angry as I was with the world, I felt a kind of peace here, a momentary easing of breath.

I remember, when we got to our destination, how the oil rig was a tiny blip in the border between sea and sky, a crooked arm raised up, a scarecrow. TundraSaur's rig was only the second major oil drilling operation in the Arctic, but the world's oil companies were desperately scrambling for permits to start drilling. Beside me on the deck, Natalia stared at the shoreline of her country, her jaw set. Her hair was streaked with gray, and there was a scar on her jawbone shaped like a sword. She had led several protests in Russia and had been in prison twice. We had barely spoken to each other for the past three days—she was angry with me for insisting I would take part in the action, and had told me horror stories of prison life. Her anger was no match for my obstinacy, although if I hadn't lied about my age, the others would not have supported me. Tentatively I reached out and pressed her hand where it clutched the railing. She didn't look at me or smile; just nodded, patted my hand, and went inside. A truce of sorts.

We laid anchor just outside Russian waters. Now the rig loomed large before us. There were four security boats reconnoitering the waters around it. Natalia spoke to them in rapid Russian over the radio. "We come in peace," she said, "to protest the drilling for oil in the Arctic. We are currently at anchor in international waters."

A man replied belligerently in Russian.

"He's just warning us we'll be arrested if we enter Russian waters," Natalia said. Now the game was afoot.

The night before the action felt to me like the last night in the world. I had volunteered to be among those courting arrest because I wanted to bring climate change to the attention of the Indian public. Although there was a national action plan on climate, the government was building coal-fired power plants as though there was no tomorrow. (With that much fossil fuel being burned, there wouldn't be). All the work of scientists like my mother, all their warnings, had gone to nothing. Reading the news about cyclones and floods, heat waves and freak storms was bad enough. When the sea came for Mumbai, breaching the new sea wall and sweeping away the familiar streets of my childhood, it brought horrors from which even Fahad

Uncle couldn't protect me. I was haunted—by my mother's eyes, when she lay dying, by the memory of walking through waist-deep flood waters, terrified I'd be swept away. In my nightmares I heard the roar of the water, felt Mona's hand slip from mine, again and again. She had been my mother's graduate student. Fahad Uncle shouted, grabbed me, made a leap for her, but the current was too strong. There were snakes in the water, and the distended bodies of slum children, and once, a pink, plastic doll with bright orange hair, smiling maniacally. Three years later there are still nights I can't sleep.

But that last night before the action, I was awake for a different reason. My responsibility was to help unleash the webstorm on the internet, an extreme cyber-weather event that would come in like a cyclone, sweeping into other conversations and connections, not by force but by the power of social media and crazy network geometry. I was crazy-network-geometry girl, on deck with my laptop and twitchy fingers, waiting for our tech team to let the drones go.

The drone lights were dimmed to a barely perceptible glow. We sent them off fondly, with a bottle or two of wine. On my screen you could see the locations of the drones, little yellow blinking lights, the seeing eyes of the world. With a touch of my finger, the Million Eyes Inner Collective around the world woke up in Dhaka and Rangoon, Boston and Vladivostok, Oslo and Berlin. Questions and answers popped on the screen like firecrackers—*We can't see anything! Well, it's night over there, moron! I see some lights! Is that the rig? No, it's effing aliens. Of course it is the rig. We go worldwide as soon as action starts in the morning.*

That morning Natalia and I, and Fabio, and Aarne went in the little boat with the banner and the megaphone. In the cold, pre-dawn light, with pink streaks in the eastern sky, the water was very still, as though the world was waiting with bated breath. We could hear, faintly, signs of early morning activity on the rig, and someone on one of the security boats calling out. Our boat was so small they didn't see us until we were quite close to the platform. We let the banner go. It rose like a ghost while Natalia worked the remote, up and up, until it made contact with the top part of the rig and stayed there. The letters were so huge that you could still see what they said from down below, in English and Russian: TundraSaur: Continuing the Proud Tradition of Destroying the Earth.

The confrontation is burned in my memory. I had expected the shouted warning, the security boat looming over us. I didn't expect that we would be so roughly treated. We were courting arrest after all. They boarded us and dragged us up onto the deck of their boat. Natalia was yelling something in Russian. Some brute put a hand on her breast and she kicked him in the groin, and then things got bloody. The man who was holding me pulled my head back by my hair, and twisted my arms around me, avoiding my kicking feet. I looked wildly around me and saw through tears that Natalia was handcuffed, blood dripping from her nose, and Aarne and Fabio were both roughed up. Fabio looked furious; Aarne had a deceptive calm on his face, a hint of triumph. He was looking at Natalia, trying to say something with his eyes, and suddenly there was an answering triumph in her own gaze that she immediately covered up. I realized it then, of course. The nearest drone, tiny, stealthy and barely visible, had video-captured everything. I looked across the expanse of sea to the distant silhouette of our little ship, and saw the glow of the signal that meant: *Webstorm Arctic Light unleashed*.

Fabio began to shout for a superior officer. His Russian is pretty good, and it helps that he looks like a bear. I couldn't understand what he was saying, or Natalia a moment later, but I knew it from our practice sessions. They were talking about the need to respect peaceful protesters' rights, but also about why we were doing what we were doing. Both Fabio and Natalia are trained in oratory—even our brutish captors stopped in their tracks for a moment. Their speeches, via their state-of-the-art wrist computers, were going out to the world in real time.

Ultimately some superior personage came and shouted at our captors and brought a doctor to attend to Natalia and Fabio (later I learned they cracked a rib of his—he was orating in quite a bit of pain). Then there was the hustle to get us to cells in the security boat, and finally to a truck on shore that would take us to the nearest big town.

That's how I ended up in prison.

*

They separated Natalia and me at once. I was shut off from the light, from the sky, from space, cramped into a cell with a woman who stared at me without comprehension. Her hair was tangled around her face—she looked prematurely aged. In all the time I was there, she didn't speak to me even once. The only noises she made were when she snored, and when she wept. In the dining halls the women laughed at my poor Russian and teased me about the "Natalia" I was seeking. The food smelled of shoe leather, and the steel doors clanged with a reverberating finality. In that cold, dark place, with the roaches and (I swear) rats running under my bunk, I had no space in my head for anything but despair and horror.

In my third month there, I got sick with a stomach bug that was going around. Tossing in my bunk, or vomiting into the toilet, I longed with feverish desperation to get out, to go back home again, to Fahad Uncle and maybe even college, and never, ever see the inside of a prison again.

The Indian consulate sent me a lawyer, a pimply fellow with sly eyes who told me my best bet was to claim I was fifteen, not twenty. I could claim, he said, that my older accomplices had deceived me, manipulated me, forced me to go with them. I'd be out of here in no time. For a moment I thought he'd guessed my age, or close to it—I was sixteen, not fifteen—but my fake passport had taken him in. I stared at him—my stomach was still not recovered, and I was queasy. He mistook my sick, dazed, half-starved look for stupidity. He told me we needed to think through it carefully—he would be back next month.

I lay in my bunk, holding my stomach and trying not to think about throwing up. I couldn't imagine freedom. My cellmate sobbed inconsolably in her bed. I screamed at her, and she stopped and looked vacantly at me. That was worse than her sobbing. I broke down and cried, and cried.

An image came to me of the first time we'd field tested one of the drones, over in Northern Canada, before we set off on the *Valiant*. The camera had captured the slow collapse of a young polar bear onto the snowy tundra where it breathed its last, frosted breaths, all skin and bone from starvation. That's how I felt now, alone in the world, without hope. There was no point in trying to do anything. My mother had been wrong in trying, and Fahad Uncle, and my friends on the *Valiant*. The oil barons were too powerful. All I had to do, when the lawyer came back, was to turn against Natalia and the others, as he'd suggested. I thought about how angry Natalia had been with me for insisting I court arrest, and wondered if she'd understand—surely she'd understand—if I betrayed them.

That night, I lay awake. There was grime on the wall by my bunk, and words scratched out in Cyrillic that I couldn't read, but I saw for the first time that someone had taken a hard object and made a crude drawing of a mountain range. It was a reminder that there was a world outside, and there were other people who re-membered. I tumbled back in my mind to a certain summer in the Himalayas, when I was thirteen years old.

*

Imagine me, a small, childish figure standing on an endless field littered with rocks and pebbles—what geologists call a moraine. It slopes up and up toward the ice wall, all the way to the distant white tongue of the glacier. I'm standing huddled in my parka against the unaccustomed cold, kicking at the rock at my feet. Fahad Uncle and his group are moving around and muttering incomprehensibly, the way scientists do when they are out in the field. This was the last glacier my mother visited before the sickness killed her a year ago. She had been determined to measure unrecorded glacier lengths in the northeastern Himalayas, but she didn't make it. She came back about halfway through the planned trip, because she was already sick. I will always remember how she would look at the sky through the hospital window—the murky, polluted city sky—but in her eyes was the light of the Himalayas, the light of sun on snow.

This is the first time her team—now Fahad Uncle's team—is visiting this glacier, locally known as the Nilsaya.

Kicking at pebbles, I feel suffused with my mother's presence. The silence here is restful, punctuated only by the muted conversations of the scientists and the distant sharp cracks and groans of the glacier. Then I see, a little ahead of me, a marker, protruding from the mess of rocks and pebbles: a metal stake and a tattered little flag atop it.

I run up to it, shouting. The marker's what they've been looking for. The place where the glacier's front edge was, two years ago, as marked by my mother on that last trip.

"Fahad Uncle! Fahad Uncle!"

He's been in my life longer than my father ever was. He's got about him a calm, silent air, rather like a mountain. He gives my shoulder a gentle victory punch as his post-doc retrieves my mother's last marker and hands it to me.

It's a solemn moment, because I am holding the last thing she touched when she was still mostly whole. But it is also a bit of a shock for us because nobody thought the glacier would have retreated this much in such a short time. Here, where we are standing at this moment, is where that distant cliff of ice was, just two years ago.

I hold the marker in my hand, and look at the glint of sun on the glacier so far up the slope. My fears rise around me in a dark wave, and the dam breaks. I weep as though I will never stop.

Fahad Uncle holds me, says, "Shaila, Shaila." What they don't know is that I am crying not only for my mother, but for the whole world.

That's when I decide: I will join the fight. That is the moment that will bring me, a few eventful years later, to the Arctic. That's before I know about prisons.

*

The lawyer didn't come back for two months, and then only because the Webstorm had finally generated enough worldwide outrage. He told me the UN had held a special session about Arctic drilling, and there were protests in the streets all over the world. In India the youth climate movement was taking off as never before—they had stalled three coal power plant projects and were clamoring for my release. My friends on the *Valiant* were on hunger strike. The lawyer related the news with an air of faint distaste, as though all this was beneath him. The thought that there were people outside trying to get me out made the tears come into my eyes. When the lawyer began outlining his strategy, I decided I hated his sly eyes and his condescension. With a spurt of my old anger I told him to get lost.

I was breathing so hard I thought I would pass out. But the anger did me some good—it cut through my despair. How I survived the remaining months I don't know, but it must have had something to do with my rage and the memory of light.

*

Yesterday they let us go. I spent eight months in a Russian prison, and my birthday present was my freedom. I stepped out of the courthouse, momentarily blinded by the brightness of the day. I breathed in great gulps of fresh air. There were red and yellow flowers blooming in the square. And there was Fahad Uncle, unfamiliar in a Russian-style hat, fighting through the crowds toward me, shouting and waving. After the tears and hugs, he handed me something.

"You should have this," he said.

I unwound the cloth from the small bundle he handed me. A battered little metal marker, the tattered flag atop it. My mother's last scientific act: the stake in the ground, the declaring of a boundary, a catastrophe, a limit. But also, maybe, a gauntlet.

We began walking together toward the taxi stand. My mobile phone (recently returned to me) beeped: a message from Captain Bill on the *Valiant*, congratulating me on my release. An unspoken question hung in the air. I thought of the sun on snow, and felt my mother beside me as though she had never left.

I took a deep breath. I would go home for a while, remember how to live in the world again. And then—

I'll be back, I texted him, and followed Fahad Uncle to the taxi.

Utopias of the Third Kind

To WRITE OF UTOPIA at this critical moment in world history—a global pandemic, the worldwide rise of totalitarian populists, the unraveling of Earth's natural cycles (resulting in ecological disasters of which climate change is one), growing social inequality, abysses of hatred opening up to divide nations and communities—to write of utopia in such a time is surely to invite allegations of pathological escapism, or perhaps some kind of delusional disorder. But could it be possible that certain kinds of utopian dreaming—on which I'll elaborate below—represent a necessary defiance, an obdurate refusal to cede space, imaginative and otherwise, to the world-destroying world-machine that is our current socioeconomic-political system? The Indian poet Sahir Ludhianvi spoke lyrically of the urgency of dreams, especially in dark times. More recently, scholars and writers such as Frederic Jameson, China Miéville and Ursula K. Le Guin have concurred, while also warning us of the pitfalls of certain conceptions of Utopia.

As an intellectual vagrant and writer of speculative fiction, I too have stumbled upon (and helped proliferate) utopias of the imagination. But as a physics professor and educator working on a transdisciplinary, justice-centered conceptualization of climate change, I'm also rooted in the real world, *this* world of ours, with all its marvels and horrors. I'm especially interested in learning how to *see* differently, to pay attention to and learn from what is pushed aside, ignored, marginalized. How do utopian yearnings manifest in the real world, with its brutal pyramidal power structures? How are these reflected (if at all) in literature now? How, in turn, might literature learn from these, and become part of social change? Can today's real-life experiments in resistance—distinctly different from those of, for example, utopian societies of North America in the nineteenth century—actually inform new ways out of our current complex of crises?

Those of us with societal privilege are relatively insulated from the worst aspects of the crises that affect othered humans and non-humans, yet it is the elite who claim to have the solutions to these problems, and the power to effect these solutions. The insularity of the privileged blinds us epistemologically as well. I have been conscious of these issues for a long time, wondering what reality looks like to those we have *othered*, how they might conceptualize such phenomena as climate change or well-being, and how that might better inform our ways ahead.

Encounters with Utopia

In the Spring of 2020, when my sabbatical in India extended due to the pandemic, I wandered, impelled by curiosity, into the virtual halls of the Seventh South South Forum on Sustainability, held at Lingnan University in Hong Kong in July 2020. Here I found accounts—from scholars and activists who serve as bridges between the privileged and the marginalized—of real-life experiments that are, in some sense utopic, or at least demonstrate utopian longings. I was familiar with some of the Indian stories: the legendary Mendha Lekha village in Maharashtra, for example, which had defeated the scourge of alcoholism, protected its forests, and its right to self-determination, and where no decision could be taken without the consensus of all men and women of the community; the extraordinary story of the Dalit women farmers of the Deccan Development society and their organic farming revolution; the resilience of the Dongria Kondh tribals in their struggle to protect their beloved Niyamgiri hills. But I only had the vaguest notion of how resistance and struggle had birthed the feminist Kurdish communities of Rojava, or the brave experiments of the Zapatistas in Mexico. And I hadn't heard before about the island of La Gomera, where sustainable practices had allowed resident farmers and their animals to become nearly self-sufficient in food, generating energy from biomass and kite technology, and growing organic food. I hadn't heard about a twenty-first-century rural reconstruction movement in China aiming to bring back vitality and resilience to the struggling countryside, seeking a new relationship between parts and whole, informed by practices such as organic agriculture and ecological farming, and rooted in cultural traditions thousands of years old that sought a healthier relationship with the rest of Nature. There were stories like these from South East Asia, Latin America, Europe, indicating the possibility of microstates of well-being amidst the despoiled social-ecological landscape of our current apocalypse.

Scholars on Utopia

After the conference I went trawling through my library and the seas of the internet to see what I could find about utopia and its manifestations. An enormous body of scholarly and literary work exists on the subject of Utopia, from Marx's critique of the naiveté of the early utopian socialists to recent work on utopian responses to colonialism. Utopia as a concept refuses to die; Even when the word *Utopia* is not mentioned, it can make its presence felt in the sense of what scholars have called "collective dreaming," a yearning for something better.

Utopia has long outgrown its original conception—the story of that name written by Sir Thomas More in 1516. As scholars have pointed out, the word itself is a pun, a grey zone between "utopia" (no-place) and "eutopia" (good place). The original meaning of a place of perfect harmony where there is no change, has given way to something broader and more complex. A wonderful bird's-eye view of the elaboration of the idea comes from Barnita Bagchi's introduction to the book *The Politics of the (Im)Possible: Utopia and Dystopia Reconsidered*, which collects essays from scholars around the globe on multiple utopian imaginaries, from feminist to Indigenous. Like Jacqueline Dutton in *The Cambridge Companion to Utopian Literature*, Bagchi argues that utopia is not limited to Europe or

European thought; Dutton advocates for the term "intercultural imaginaries of the ideal." Lyman Tower Sargent, in his essay "The Necessity of Utopian Thinking: A Cross-National perspective," in the volume *Thinking Utopia: Steps into Other Worlds*, points out that many countries have rich and complex traditions of utopian literature. In the same volume, Zhang Longxi, detailing the utopian tradition in Chinese literature, quotes Ruth Levitas as saying that a utopia is a social construct, a response to an equally socially constructed gap perceived between the current and the ideal.

The broadening of the notion of Utopia from static perfection to something more complex, more paradoxical and wide-ranging—a collective desire for a better social arrangement—allows for a proliferation of classifications and categories. Writers too have added to the taxonomy; consider, for instance Le Guin's yang and yin utopias. Of special interest to me is the notion that the experience of colonialism gives rise to utopian dreaming—including settler utopias, which are, as Lyman Tower Sargent notes, the colonialists' dreams of a new and better world than the home they left, to be contrasted with the desire for freedom and self-determination that is the response of the colonized people. Sandeep Banerjee, in *Space, Utopia and Indian Decolonization*, further subdivides the latter category, the utopias of the colonized, into anticolonial nationalist imaginings, which may be quite reactionary, and the open, contested, pluralistic space of decolonization. Of particular relevance to the talks I attended at Lingnan University is Anupama Mohan's work *Utopia and the Village in South Asian Literature*, in which the village in India and Sri Lanka is examined as a site of both a pastoral utopia and a dystopia. Among other things, Mohan examines village-as-utopia in Gandhi's *Hind Swaraj*, which led to literary, social-theoretic and on-the-ground experiments, anticolonial responses to British occupation. Rather like Banerjee, she divides literary utopias into two kinds: the homotopia, which is a vision of unified collectivity motivated by aggressive exclusion on the basis of some ideology, caste, or religion, and the pluralistic, open visions inspired by Gandhi and Tagore.

Interestingly, while declaring literary utopias to be a lost cause, Krishan Kumar mentions one kind of real-world utopia that has not, according to him, as yet found its theoreticians or chroniclers. He uses the term "glocalization," attributed to Roland Robertson, to describe a kind of present-day utopianism that is distinct from the experiments of the past, in which small, locally grounded practices of better ways of living are also consciously global in seeking and accepting influence, resources and insights. He does not elaborate, nor does he mention the Vikalp Sangam Project or the Global tapestry of Alternatives, but several of the stories I heard from scholars and activists at the SSFS7 conference would fit his description of a glocalized utopia.

Utopias of the Third Kind

As someone born, raised and formed in a country that was colonized by the British for two hundred years, I am especially interested in utopian imagination as a response to colonialism. As Lyman Tower Sargent points out, there are two kinds of colonialism, broadly speaking—settler colonialism (North American and Australian) and the kind in which resource exploitation is the key motivation (such as India under British rule), although you can also have something in between. Each gives rise to its own visions of a "better future." Of the responses to colonialism, I enumerate three. One is a reactionary, exclusionary, nationalistic response that looks backward to a conveniently edited golden past, and seeks to recreate it in the present, usually by excluding not only the colonizers but any group considered inconvenient for the project. It is based on manufactured pride and a masculinist hubris concealing a deep insecurity, a sense of not being good enough. This is the kind of utopia that—especially if it is conceived by a socially privileged group in a diverse society—depends on the coexistence of dystopias for multiple others. However much it might seek to idealize existence for its preferred citizens within its borders, it has boundary lines of hate and exclusion. A second response to colonialism is a vision that seeks to emulate the values, technologies, and social systems of the colonizers, to best them on their terms, eschewing precolonial knowledges, histories, and epistemologies in favor of modernity. This is an aspect of sociologist Anibal Quijano's notion of coloniality of power, referring to the way that colonial power structures cement racial hierarchies and enable epistemic and cultural dominance, even when the colonizers are far away. Here also a key affective component is shame—a feeling of not being worthy, or being backward. These are, of course, at extreme ends of a continuum—a hybrid of the two is quite possible. What unites the two kinds of utopian visions—exclusionary/reactionary and mimetic/modernist is this: they are both responses to colonization in which the colonizer remains the unit of comparison.

> Where the mind is without fear and the head is held high
> Where knowledge is free
> Where the world has not been broken up into fragments
> By narrow domestic walls
> Where words come out from the depth of truth
> Where tireless striving stretches its arms towards perfection
> Where the clear stream of reason has not lost its way
> Into the dreary desert sand of dead habit . . .

So the poet and Nobel Laureate Rabindranath Tagore sang of a very different conception of India. Tagore opposed British rule and was critical of nationalism as a modernist construct but also critiqued Indian social norms and hierarchies. Could there be, then, a third response to colonialism, one that frees us from the standards and measures of the colonizing power?

Rabindranath composed his hopeful paean to the India of the future before the British left. But we don't simply live in countries—countries are socially constructed abstractions, as any view of Earth from space will tell us. We live in places. Writing the first draft of this essay near Delhi, there I was, with the mango tree outside the window, the warbler singing in the bushes, the vegetable seller pushing his cart on the road outside, calling. We are local beings, yet we are inevitably connected to the rest of the planet, indebted to planet-spanning, life-maintaining processes and cycles. The molecules in the breath I've just taken now, were, a year or two ago, expelled from the blowhole of a bowhead whale in the Arctic, mingled with those in a hot Saharan wind, and the exhalation of the Amazon rainforest. In premodern times, we could be content with being local, living in small settlements or as hunter-gatherers deeply connected to our environs. In this moment of multiple planetary crises, we must come to the realization that we are simultaneously local and planetary.

Utopias of the third kind—as I conceive them—are visions that are grounded in the local, in its geography and social-cultural-ecological surround, but locate themselves in a planetary context, where "local" and "planetary" are not mutually exclusive categories but are connected in space and time. More often than not, such utopias result from struggle, resistance, and the kind of imaginative creativity that is best forged by those exploited and exiled by the systems of power. This third response to colonialism—whether settler colonialism or resource-extractive colonialism at a distance—questions not only the paradigms of the colonizers but also those of one's own culture and history, and values aspects of both. Nor does such a response limit itself solely to the axis of colonizer-colonized, but learns from other cultures and peoples of the various ways of being. Such a response is not static or rigid, but always learning, always in a process of adjustment and change. This curious, critical, playful, open examination of possibilities within and beyond the experience of colonization seems to me to be the most freeing.

Of course, this "definition" of Utopias of the Third Kind is very general, so I will focus on a subset of this category in which I am most interested, one which is distinguished by a radical egalitarianism. Even when there is some degree of homogeneity due to historical reasons, for example in tribal communities, the boundary lines of such utopias as I imagine them are not demarcated by hatred and distrust of difference. Where communities are plural, this entails a fellow feeling that transcends religious and gender differences. Self-determination and participatory democracy are key, and consensus rather than majority voting are how decisions are taken. Nor are such utopias prescriptive—they embrace humility as a key principle that enables them to evolve organically and syncretically, weaving their ideas from experience, and their experience from ideas, always in relation to each other and the rest of Nature. Such utopias are not perfect—if utopia is a desire or a transformative impulse, then we can think of it as a direction rather than a destination. Utopias of the third kind are always becoming, always changing, edging only asymptotically toward whatever the ever-changing socially constructed definition of the ideal society might be. And while such a utopia in one part of the world is necessarily different from one in another (as different as Mendha Lekha and Chiapas, for example), they would, in my conception, share a planetary consciousness. My description is similar to Ursula K. Le Guin's yin utopias and Krishan Kumar's notion of the glocalized utopia, but is a little more specific.

Localized utopias (of the third kind) are perhaps the only real utopias possible, because geography, culture, history and the local manifestations of oppression shape, in part, how people conceive and build their ideals of the best life. So utopias, then, must be different from each other, yet their global expression must have weight, if we are to dislodge the global pyramid of power that has such a hold on our imaginations and our lives. How?

It is largely to find the answer to this question that I've been following for some years the Vikalp Sangam project and the Global Tapestry of Alternatives, which compile in detail the many different experiments in resistance and alternative living and being that are taking place around the world. In order to counter the paralysis of the imagination, we need three interrelated things: first, proof-of-concept experiments that are grounded in reality, which counter the paradigm of destructive "development" of modern industrial civilization. Second, stories, old and new, informed by these experiments but also freed by the imagination. We are a storytelling species, after all. Narrativizing is what we do to co-construct and make sense of reality. Third, underlying all these is the need for different paradigms, onto-epistemologies, ways of seeing the world that free us from the trap of the imagination.

The real-life stories that I find most inspiring are characterized first of all by value systems and epistemologies that are noncapitalist: that is, important aspects of life, such as well-being: physical material and environmental, are not subject to commodification, nor is the market the model for life and living. Instead of an exclusive focus on the individual, or the pressure to conform to social norms under threat, we have individual freedom *and* social good through a sense of heightened responsibility to each other, expressed in such concepts as "ubuntu," "buen vivir," and "ecological swaraj" or "radical ecological democracy." Individual agency and a deep social-ecological responsibility are not counter to each other, but reinforce each other in these societies. Thus such societies tend to have flattened hierarchies socially and politically. For example, in the village of Mendha Lekha, women have as much say in village decisions as men. And because every individual is important, the village works by consensus, not majority vote. Another key aspect of such utopias is the relationship between humans and the rest of Nature. Modern industrial civilization is founded on an exploitative relationship with other species, and an illusory separation of the human and natural. No value is given to the lives and survival of nonhuman beings. Contrast this with the Dongria Kondh people, who, when offered compensation packages to relocate so that their hills could be mined and their forests destroyed, asked "But what about the animals?" By considering themselves as part of the web of life, these communities have, over millennia of interacting with other species, developed sophisticated knowledge systems allowing them to interpret, affect, and be affected by the environment in ways that urban humans can barely begin to imagine. This also implies a concept of sufficiency, a respect for limits of natural reserves and processes, in striking contrast with the idea of endless economic growth that fuels the consumerism of modern industrial civilization. The related idea that most basic needs should be met locally is also a feature of these utopias. Thus food sovereignty, access to water and forest produce, and legal rights, especially collective rights to the land, are important to the long-term sustainability of these microcosms. All of this results in people who are actively engaged in their communities, always learning, leading lives of self-respect and dignity without exploiting others.

Time and Utopia

Beneath my exploration of different kinds of utopia is a certain implicit assumption that illuminates the need for alternate epistemologies: that of the nature of time. Linear time as an absolute concept is part of the Western Newtonian or mechanistic paradigm, and unfortunately it informs how we think about things well beyond the domain of validity of Newtonian physics. Time is a slippery concept, a fact that physicists recognize, but linear time is entrenched in modern industrial civilization in especially damaging ways. Consider the ubiquity of such actions as setting goals and determining straight-line pathways toward them, even when situations are complex and demand a model of constant engagement and adaptive responses. Consider the compartmentalization of time in one's daily schedule. Many cultures have alternative views of time in addition to linear time that recognize, for example, the prevalence of cycles. My own fascination with time has led me to speculate on its peculiar porous, fractal qualities by way of speculative fiction. However, a particularly clarifying and relevant view of time comes from Indigenous Potawatomi scholar Kyle Whyte's essays, "Time as Kinship" and "Against Crisis Epistemologies." In these he first talks about the way climate science tells the story of climatic changes on the planet—one that I am quite familiar with in my academic work as a physicist-transdisciplinary scholar of climate change—as a series of unfolding events and processes leading us to inevitable catastrophe. This is, of course, literally the case, especially in the absence of meaningful action. Whyte points out that this leads to fear as a natural reaction, which can be co-opted by the powers-that-be to push harmful technological "solutions" on us that hurt marginalized people and the environment. From my own readings about the brain and trauma, it seems also that when we experience deep fear, our prefrontal cortex, the seat of logical and complex thinking, tends to go offline.

But Whyte goes further. Through various tellings of the climate story from Indigenous perspectives, he brings out the contrast—Indigenous narratives of climate change are stories about changes in kinship relationships, where kin are all we are connected to, not just biological relations—thus trees, rocks, ants, birds. In this telling the climate crisis is a story of changing and ultimately broken relationships between kin. The implication is clear—what we need is to mend and heal these broken relationships. Of course some aspects of the healing will involve technology, but imagine the *kinds* of technology that might arise from such a perspective! Such an *epistemology of coordination*, to use Whyte's term, cannot make the fatal error of simply substituting fossil fuel infrastructure with green energy, nor can it endorse the displacement of Indigenous people from their lands for a wind farm, or permit the mining of the ocean for minerals for electric vehicles. This way of seeing, when made real through collective responsibility and alternate models of governance, allows us to transcend the false dichotomies of capitalist modernity: individual/collective, human/nature, economy/ecology, to name a few.

Thus, as I see it from reading these essays, our work in the world is to recognize broken relationships at every scale and context, and to collectively and responsibly engage in the work of healing and mending, thereby allowing for our own healing. Such a process is also a response to urgency, but, I suspect, has a better chance at actually working than the fear-driven violence of solutions emerging from the linear time narrative. Thinking about this in relation to my conception of utopias of the Third Kind, it seems to me that this view of time—as the flow of kinship relationships—is already prevalent in some of the real-world utopias I have described, and the people in these places are already engaged in the work of reweaving the world from where they are. The metaphor of weaving is particularly natural for me, having grown up with the songs of the fifteenth-century Indian mystic poet and weaver Kabir, so it makes sense to me that we are weaving the world and simultaneously being woven by it, into being, into change! And this leads me to another realization, that proto-utopias of the Third Kind may sometimes exist here and now without our noticing—in temporal, embryonic ways, in small spacetime pockets even in colonial and capitalist spaces. These pocket proto-utopias, at once individual and collective, exist briefly in the places and moments when we sense—when *we make and are made by*—the relationships that make the world whole. They are fleeting, being temporally as well as spatially bound (my inner particle physicist is reminded of virtual particles of the submicrocosm that pop in and out of existence!). What can we do to incubate these spacetime pocket proto-utopias? To grow them into something that has weight in the world? As raindrops coalesce on a windowpane, perhaps we need to connect these fleeting glimpses of utopias with the ones already in the making around the world. Keep weaving, keep weaving.

Speculative Fiction and Utopias of the Third Kind

I am not sure to what extent speculative fiction has engaged in describing and exploring utopias of the third kind. There has certainly been plenty of exploration of a specific utopia grounded in a place, but what of a constellation of micro-utopias, each different from the other, yet connected via a planetwide network? According to Krishan Kumar, such fictive explorations don't exist, but, being merely a writer, I will leave it to scholars to decide.

What I can say as a writer is that speculative fiction is ideal for examining utopias of the third kind. Humans are storytellers. The power of speculative fiction is to invoke narrative to immerse us in worlds where things aren't the same as the world or worlds in which we live. There is surely no more revolutionary a question than "what if things were not as they are?" By imagining the multitude of answers to such "what-if" questions, speculative fiction has the potential to free us from the trap of the imagination I call the reality trap. The reality trap binds us to our current ways of life, and enables our continuing servitude to power hierarchies by asserting that only what is real now—"real" defined by the dominant modes of thinking—informs the possibilities of the future. Speculative fiction can take direct inspiration from real-life experiments that challenge and complicate the dominant notion of what's real and possible. I imagine a positive (in all senses) feedback loop between such a literature and the material possibilities on the ground, each inspiring and being inspired by the other. May the world-destroying world-machine that has us in its thrall find within it the seeds, not just of its own destruction, but of multiple, viable, alternative worlds.

Bibliography

Bagchi, Barnita, ed. *The Politics of the (Im)Possible: Utopia and Dystopia Reconsidered.* New Delhi: Sage Publications, 2019.

Banerjee, Sandeep. *Space, Utopia and Indian Decolonization: Literary Prefigurations of the Postcolony.* London: Routledge, 2019.

Claeys, Gregory, ed. *The Cambridge Companion to Utopian Literature.* Cambridge Companions to Literature. Cambridge: Cambridge University Press, 2010.

Global Tapestry of Alternatives. https://globaltapestryofalternatives.org/.

Hébert, Martin. "Worlds Not Yet in Being." *Anthropology & Materialism* no. 3 (2016). https://journals.openedition.org/am/604.

Jameson, Fredric. *Archaeologies of the Future.* London: Verso, 2005.

Kumar, Krishan. "The Ends of Utopia—Krishan Kumar." *New Literary History* 41, no. 3 (Summer 2010): 549–69.

Le Guin, Ursula K. "Ursula Le Guin Explains How to Build a New Kind of Utopia." Electric Lit,

December 5, 2017. https://electricliterature.com/ursula-k-le-guin-explains-how-to-build-a-new-kind-of-utopia/.

Miéville, China. "The Limits of Utopia." Salvage, 2015. https://salvage.zone/mieville_all.html.

Mohan, Anupama. *Utopia and the Village in South Asian Literature.* London: Palgrave Macmillan, 2012.

Rüsen, Jörn., Michael Fehr, Thomas Rieger, eds. *Thinking Utopia: Steps into Other Worlds.* Oxford: Berghahn Books, 2005.

Sargent, Lyman Tower. "Utopian Literature in English: An Annotated Bibliography from 1516 to the Present." University Park, PA: Penn State Libraries Open Publishing, 2016 and continuing. https://openpublishing.psu.edu/utopia/

Seventh South South Forum on Sustainability at Lingnan University. Conference website with links to specific talks and essays https://www.ln.edu.hk/events/seventh-south-south-forum-on-sustainability-climate-change-global-crises-and-community-regeneration.

Smith, Eric D. *Globalization, Utopia and Postcolonial Science Fiction: New Maps of Hope.* London: Palgrave Macmillan, 2014.

Vikalp Sangam Project. https://vikalpsangam.org/. See also Global Tapestry of Alternatives.

Whyte, Kyle Powys. "Time as Kinship." In *The Cambridge Companion to Environmental Humanities.* Edited by Jeffrey Cohen and Stephanie Foote. Cambridge: Cambridge University Press, 2021.

———. "Against Crisis Epistemologies." In *Handbook of Critical Indigenous Studies*, edited by Brendan Hokowhitu, Aileen Moreton-Robinson, Linda Tuhiwai-Smith, Steve Larkin, and Chris Andersen. London: Routledge, 2020. https://kylewhyte.cal.msu.edu/wp-content/uploads/sites/12/2020/07/Whyte-Against-Crisis-Epistemology-2020-1.pdf.

Hunger

SHE WOKE UP EARLY as usual. The apartment, with its plump sofas like sleeping walruses, the pictures on the walls slightly and mysteriously askew, pale light from the windows glinting off yesterday's glasses she'd forgotten on the coffee table—the apartment seemed as though it had been traveling through alien universes all night and had only now landed in this universe, cautiously letting in the unfamiliar air. Outside the birds were stirring, parakeets in the neem trees, mynahs strutting on the roadsides, their calls mingling with the beep beep beep of a car backing up in the parking area below.

How strange everything was! In the dream last night it had been the most natural thing in the world to be dancing with a tree, to be nibbling gently at the red fruit hanging from its branches as they swayed. Vikas hadn't been with her in that dream, and she had felt slightly guilty dancing with someone else, even in a dream, even if that someone had been a tree that could walk. But it had seemed so natural, so familiar, that in that moment she'd been convinced, finally, that she had found her home planet. And just as she'd started feeling at home, her eyes had opened, and there she was, lying in a strange bed next to a strange beast that she slowly recognized as her very dear husband, Vikas.

And where have *you* been? she wanted to ask him, but he was asleep. If she told him her dream he would laugh and threaten to find a shrink. Not for you, Divya, he would say, but for me. He liked to say that she was beyond redemption, reading those trashy science fiction novels. But sometimes she wanted to ask him quite seriously how to explain the way she felt in the mornings: that even the most familiar thing felt strange, that she had to—almost—learn the world anew. Try explaining that! she said to Vikas's imaginary shrink.

Their daughter lay asleep in her room, curled like an embryo among the sheets. She was twelve today, there was going to be a big party, what was she, Divya, doing, standing in the doorway of the child's room, thinking about alien universes! The child herself—how much longer a child? So strange, so different from the squalling, wrinkled little creature she had first held in her arms twelve years ago! Her face still so young, so innocent, yet on the inside she was developing layers, convolutions; she was becoming someone that Divya as yet did not know. Divya sighed and went out of the room, drifting through the apartment, touching and straightening things as though to make sure they were there, they were fine. She picked up the glasses from the coffee table and went into the kitchen, which (being on the northwest side of the apartment) was still in darkness. With the usual trepidation she turned on the light.

As light flooded the room, mice fled to dark corners. Divya stepped gingerly in. The kitchen was never hers at night but belonged, for that duration, to the denizens of another world. There were cockroach cocktail parties and mouse reunions, and (in the monsoons) conferences of lost frogs. In the kitchen sink, the nali-ka-kida, the drain insects, whatever they were, waited hopefully for darkness, waving their feelers. None of the other creatures—mice and muskrats and frogs—bothered Divya like the cockroaches and nali-ka-kida. But it unnerved her that she had somehow, quite unknowingly, surrendered ownership of the kitchen at night.

She put the glasses noisily in the sink. Kallu the crow flew down to the windowsill from the neem tree outside, and cawed at her. His presence was a relief. She gave him a piece of the paratha that she had been saving up from last night to eat later. The parathas were fat, stuffed with spiced potatoes and peas, the best that the cook Damyanti had ever made. For a moment Divya wanted desperately to curl up in bed with the parathas and a book with a title like "The Aliens of Malgudi" or "Antariksh ki Yatra." The day stretched before her, rife with impossibilities—to get all that food cooked, the whole house cleaned, and then to entertain the families of Vikas's colleagues without a faux pax . . . It simply couldn't be done. She wasn't made for such things—she was from another planet, where you danced with trees and ate parathas and read trashy science fiction novels.

But it had to be done. "Take me with you, Kallu," she told the crow, but he only cawed sardonically at her and flew heavily off. She sighed and began to wash the glasses. If only Vikas hadn't got-ten that big promotion, she thought, feeling guilty for thinking so. Now he was junior vice president, which was not at all as exciting as a president of vices ought to be—and they had to move amongst the upper echelons of the company, VPs and CEOs, whose houses were completely air-conditioned and windows all shut, so that mice and cockroaches and frogs would have to line up and come in at the main entrance, with the permission of the doorkeeper, like everybody else. The most innocent of things, like children's birthdays, were now minor political extravaganzas with the women all made up, clinking with expensive jewelry, sniping gently at each other while calling each other "darling," and the men talking on like robots about stocks and shares.

She went to the back door and found the newspaper on the landing. As she straightened she smelled it—a stench rolling down from the top of the stairs. The pungent, sharp, stale odor of urine.

The old man was responsible for the smell. He lived on the top landing, which was little used because it led to the rooftop terrace. Divya looked at the door of the servants' flat. It was shut tight. So was the door of the apartment opposite hers, where the morose and silent Mr. Kapadia lived. She took a deep breath and knocked loudly on the servant quarter door, where Ranu, Mr. Kapadia's cook, lived with her husband.

The woman herself opened the door. She turned her nose up at the smell.

"All right, all right," she spat, before Divya could say a word. She turned and yelled for her husband. "Wash the stairs, you lazy lout, that good-for-nothing fellow has wet his bed again!" She looked at Divya, hands on hips, nostrils flared.

"Satisfied?"

"Why don't you let the old man use the bathroom in the night?" Divya said angrily. "The poor fellow is your father-in-law—treat him with some respect! And listen, make sure the stairs stay clean all day. We have people coming over!"

In answer Ranu slammed the door. Divya went back into the house, feeling sick. She wondered if the old fellow was ill again. She let him run little errands for her, like getting the milk from the milk booth in the mornings, for which she would give him a little money or food. He was a small, thin, emaciated, birdlike man, with a slurred speech that had resulted from some disease of his middle age. Sometimes he would tell her stories of his bygone days and she would nod at intervals although she hardly understood any of it, except a word here or there, like bicycle, or river, or tomato chutney, which, put together, made no sense at all. In her more fanciful moments she had thought that perhaps the old fellow was an alien, speaking to her in an exotic tongue or in code, delivering a message that she had to try to decipher. But he was just an old man down on his luck, with no place to go but the nest of rags at the top of the stairs, subject always to the whims and frightful temper of his daughter-in-law. Divya resolved that later on she would find out if the fellow had fallen ill. He hadn't come by yesterday for the milk. She would have to send Vikas to the milk booth today.

*

Divya was hungry.

She had been cleaning all morning and had skipped lunch. By the afternoon, the house was sparkling. She hadn't known what to do with most of the things that they had accumulated—the piles of books on the floor all over the house, the loose photographs on every surface like schools of dead fish, the magazines sliding off stacks in the bathroom. But she had found in herself unexpected reserves of cunning—she'd hidden piles of books behind the beds in the bedrooms, given the magazines to the kabari man without asking Vikas if he wanted to keep any of them, collected the photos and put them in a plastic bag in the clothes cupboard. The cleaning woman, who was lazier than a street dog in the sun, loved parties and had worked with great enthusiasm to make the floors shine, knowing that some of the good food would come her way later on.

Late afternoon, Divya was standing in front of the stove, stirring the matar paneer. There was sweat gathering on her forehead, under the hairline, and steam rising off the big karhai as the peas bubbled in their sauce of onions, ginger, tomatoes, cumin, and coriander. Big chunks of paneer like white barges in the gravy, and the aroma! The aroma was enough to make the head swim. Divya had never been so hungry, and was regretting not having had lunch. She was paying for it now: her stomach rumbled, her mouth watered, she felt faint with desire. It should have been easy to munch something while cooking.

But the fact was that she was afraid of the cook. Damyanti was a small, stern woman who stood no nonsense from her employers. She took great pride in her creations and had, Divya thought, an unreasonable code of conduct: you did not eat before your guests, you did not filch from the serving dishes, and there was no need to taste the food unless you wanted to insult the cook. Damyanti had already scolded her once for trying to throw away the carrot tops.

"You've left so much of the carrots on this, I can easily take it home and put it in a sabzi; and the greens can go to Karan's cow. Don't you know what happens to those who waste food?"

The reason Damyanti could bully her employers and get away with it was because her cooking was sublime. She had condescended to stay and cook for much of the afternoon, and this meant that Divya was, by tacit agreement, completely under her thumb.

"What happens?" Divya asked, trying to sound unconcerned.

"People who waste food end up being reborn as nali-ka-kidas," said Damyanti, setting hot onion pakoras into a cloth-lined serving dish. Divya shivered. Imagine that, having those horrible, long feelers, living in dark drains, emerging at night to eat the leavings of others!

The matar paneer was done; Damyanti was setting up the big dekchi for the rice, putting in the ghee, the cardamom, a cinnamon stick, cloves. It smelled like heaven. Divya clutched the wall with one hand. The thought occurred to her that she should let the party go to hell, dismiss Damyanti and sit on the kitchen floor, surrounded by vats of fragrant dishes, and fall upon them in a frenzy. She collected herself. Maybe she should simply go get the parathas she had been saving in the fridge. They would taste divine, even cold. She had surely never been so hungry as now!

But Damyanti (coming to get the dhania leaves) caught her at the fridge, with her hand clutching a piece of paratha halfway to her mouth.

"Chee chee!" she said. "Don't you know what happens to the woman who eats during cooking? Do you want to make all the food jootha?"

Divya never found out what terrible fate would have resulted from her almost-lapse because at that precise moment Vikas came in with the cake, laughing and trying to fend Charu off because she wanted to see what it looked like. Divya had to put the parathas back and make room in the fridge for the enormous cake. Vikas touched Divya's disheveled hair as she turned away—she suppressed a desire to bite his hand.

"Are you going to face the guests like this, Divu? They'll be here in an hour! Go dress!"

"I have to get the chholey cooking," she said irritably, following Damyanti into the kitchen. There was a knock on the back door.

"I'll see who it is!" Charu said, flying off resplendent in a new blue dress, happy because the cake was her favorite kind, triple chocolate. Divya went back into the kitchen, got the other karhai on the stove, put in the oil and the spices and the onions. When Damyanti's back was turned for half a second she popped a piece of paneer into her mouth from the dish of matar paneer, and burned her mouth. She could hear Charu talking to someone at the door, running into the house and back to the door again; she heard the soft, hesitant, mangled words of the old man upstairs. So he was up and about, the old fraud! Pissing in his bed, stinking up the stairs, giving her a headache first thing in the morning! And she had had to get the milk herself earlier, because Vikas had to go out to get the drinks! Tears welled up in her eyes. If only she could eat something! How absurd this was, to be afraid to eat in your own house!

She was about to purloin another piece of paneer, burned mouth or no, when Vikas came in.

"Divya, you'll never believe what I saw in our room! A mouse! Really, when will you stop feeding every living creature in the area! They think our house is a hotel! And we have all these people coming . . . where did you put the rat poison?"

He had gotten it last week, a small blue vial of death that she hadn't been able to bring herself to use. It stood on the highest shelf in their bathroom.

"It wasn't there," he said when she told him this. "Divya, really!"

He knew she didn't like using the poison, but the traps they had used hadn't worked either. Vikas had taken the traps to the park every morning and let the mice out, but they had wasted no time in returning. Stricter measures had been called for.

What Divya remembered was this: she was ten years old, and had been visiting an aunt's house in the summer. It was an old bungalow, ridden with denizens of all kinds, including an army of mice. Her uncle had set poisoned food all over the house and killed off the army. Divya had a vivid memory of the tiny corpses, their bodies twisted with the final agony, all over the house. Then, a day or two later, there had been the smell in her room, which had finally been traced to a nest behind the big wooden cupboard. Twelve baby mice, pink and hairless, had died of starvation after the adults had been killed. All the time Divya had been reading her mystery books and sipping her lemonade, those babies had been dying slowly. She had cried for days.

"Vikas, this is no time to be setting out rat poison," she said, but he was already distracted by the pakoras. "Smells good," he said wistfully, leaning over the glass-covered dish.

Before Divya could utter a word, Damyanti had put two pakoras and some tamarind chutney on a plate and handed it to him, all the while smiling approvingly as Vikas ate. Divya stared at him, and then at her, speechless with indignation.

"But . . ." she started to say, when she heard the fridge door open and shut and there was Charu walking past the kitchen door in her blue dress, holding Divya's precious parathas in her hand.

In an instant she was in front of her daughter, confronting her, snatching the parathas away. She stared at Charu, breathless with anger.

"What are you doing with my parathas?"

Charu stared back, eyes wide with confusion.

"I was just giving it to the old man. He said he was hungry, Ma . . ."

There was a roaring in Divya's ears. She felt momentarily dizzy.

"Tell him we can't spare any," she said, more harshly than she had intended. "Don't you have better things to do? Where are the presents you were wrapping for your friends? Did you get enough for the other children too?"

An expression she could not identify flickered over the child's face. Divya knew Charu was not happy about the other children, the strangers who would be coming to the party. Apart from Charu's three friends there would be a fourteen-year-old boy, the nephew of Vikas's new boss, Mr. Lamba, and an eleven-year-old girl, daughter of the Pathanias. But all that—the sulks and protestations—had been over and done with, or so Divya thought. She saw the tears rise in Charu's eyes.

"It's my birthday," the child said, fiercely. "You're not supposed to scold me on my birthday!"

At that moment Divya was aware that certain knots had come into being in the smooth tapestry of her life, knots she would not necessarily know how to untangle, but there was Vikas calling out that the Chaturvedis were already here, and Charu was already at the door, talking to the old man. Damyanti took the parathas from Divya's limp fingers and pushed her, not ungently, in the direction of the bedroom.

"Get ready for your guests. I'll do the chholey," she said, and Divya went to change her sari and wash her face, and put on some lipstick, feeling dazed, feeling as though something momentous had happened or was about to happen. The book she was reading, *The Aliens of Malgudi*, lay on the dressing table; she stared wistfully at the lurid cover, with the spaceship and the buxom space-bandit Viraa. The plot had to do with Viraa discovering aliens disguised as humans, living in the town of Malgudi. They were from some planet light-years away. Divya wondered how she was going to survive.

As for the Chaturvedis, she should have remembered from the gossip that they always came at least half an hour early, possibly because Mrs. Chaturvedi—an inveterate gossip and interlocutor—liked to have her victims to herself before the others came.

*

The party was in full swing. Divya dashed from kitchen to drawing room, from guest to guest, until the world became a blur of silk sarees and lipsticked mouths opening and closing, the clink of glasses; the flow of myriad streams of conversations, none of which made any sense to her. In the kitchen she took a moment to wipe her brow. Just then Mrs. Lamba loomed large in the kitchen doorway, resplendent in green silk.

"My dear, what a lot of trouble! Look at you, all sweating! You should have got the whole thing catered. I will give you my caterer's telephone number. He does some very nice European-style hors d'oeuvres . . ."

"Aha, but Mrs. Lamba, you must try these pakoras . . ." Mrs. Raman said brightly, munching away behind her. Mrs. Lamba condescended to nibble at one.

"Not bad," she said in a surprised tone. Damyanti, wiping the serving dish for the chholey, glared at her.

Vikas came in wanting more glasses. There weren't enough at the bar. The Saikias and the Bhosles were here. And where was the fruit juice for the children?

Over the next hour or so, Divya caught a few glimpses of her daughter. Charu wouldn't look at her. The girl's laugh was higher than usual—she was in the middle of her little circle of friends. At the periphery were the eleven-year-old daughter of the Pathanias and the fourteen-year-old nephew of the Lambas. Divya went over to make sure they weren't feeling left out. No, Charu was nothing if not kind-hearted—she had served birthday cake to everyone, and now the two had been invited to play a computer game in Charu's room along with the inner circle of friends, and they were all trooping off together. The Lambas' nephew looked frankly bored; the Ramans' daughter cast a despairing glance at her parents as she left the room.

So much unhappiness, Divya thought suddenly. She was feeling better, with some pakoras in her stomach, but now a wave of anguish swept through her. She looked at the women, clustered together, their face paint standing out garishly in the light. It was one of those moments when everyone had run out of conversation at the same time, like actors taking a break from their roles. Mrs. Lamba's fleshy face looked haggard, Mrs. Raman's, nervous. In that moment she had a sudden shock of recognition, a fellow-feeling she could not explain. Then Mrs. Chaturvedi leaned toward Mrs. Lamba with a conspiratorial look, and the buzz of conversation resumed. What were they hatching now? Whose reputation was being built up, or destroyed? By contrast the men seemed less sinister, talking in loud voices about the latest financial news—they were like little puppets, moving and twitching to order, while the women, with Mrs. Lamba at the center, controlled the strings. Why had Divya had that sudden moment of empathy with the women—no, empathy was too strong a word—but why she had felt what she felt, she did not know.

She had a sudden longing for the days when Vikas was still a junior manager in the company and birthdays, and life itself, were less complicated. Then, she could ensure everyone's happiness. Charu could be comforted with a hug. But look at her now, with that veil over her eyes, taking a tray of soda to her room for her friends. She didn't like the way I snapped at her, Divya thought. On her birthday too! She's getting all sensitive and dignified now. Every year she steps away from me, one step. Two steps. And look at Vikas! He looked the genial host, pouring the drinks, laughing at Mr. Lamba's jokes, but she could see the strain on his face. Her poor Vikas, growing up, growing old. Worried about creating the right impression. The old Vikas had enjoyed making cartoons of his superiors, shared jokes with her about how stupid office politics was. She felt sorry for him, having to laugh at those jokes of Mr. Lamba.

What was the point of it all?

As the evening wore on, she knew that she had achieved some degree of success. Damyanti had left around the middle of the evening and she had managed the serving of the dinner mostly on her own, with some help from Mrs. Bhosle and Mrs. Raman, two ladies on the outer perimeter of Mrs. Lamba's circle. Whether it was Damyanti's cooking or whether Mrs. Lamba had been feeling indulgent, she felt as though she had passed some kind of test, that she had crossed an invisible barrier and was now one of Them. She didn't like it, didn't like pretending to like it. She wasn't as good at acting as the other women. But for Vikas . . . she looked across at him, and he raised his head and met her gaze, and in his look was relief and humor and the reassurance that the evening would soon be over. Yes, she would do it for him. At least for another half an hour, or however long it took for the last glasses to be set down, the last goodbyes said.

Then she heard a child scream.

The children had been running around, playing some kind of crazy game, after having sat still through dinner. The Lambas' nephew, Ajeet, had started them on it, Divya thought, against Charu's wishes. But he had the authority of being fourteen and having traveled all over the world with his parents (his speech was peppered with references to London and New York and Sydney), and he was already beginning to develop an air of studied cynicism, a man of the world. Divya could sense Charu being pulled in, and repelled, and pulled in, and repelled, and had suffered for her daughter, who still would not look at her. She wanted to tell her that the world wouldn't care for her hurt feelings, that she needed to be stronger and less vulnerable to everyday hurts if she were to survive; she wanted to tell her that kind of men that grew from boys like Ajeet were bad news, all preening, fake charm, and pretended indifference . . . look at him, manipulating the younger ones just because he was bored and wanted whatever entertainment the situation had to offer.

In the split second after the scream Divya established that it was not her Charu, and that the sound came from outside the apartment, from the vicinity of the back door. She was already moving toward it, and so was Vikas, and Mrs. Pathania, whose daughter it was who had screamed. At the back door she saw that the children were clustered at the top of the stairs that led to the terrace; there was a faint smell in the air, not urine. The landing was very quiet, with only one light burning over the stairway, and the servants' quarter door (she noted as she ran up the stairs) was locked.

The children moved aside to let her see; Mrs. Pathania's daughter was already half-falling down the stairs into her mother's arms. What Divya saw was the old man curled up in a nest of rags, clutching his throat with both hands, quite dead. His hooked nose, protruding from his too-thin face, gave him the appearance of a strange bird; his heavy-lidded eyes were open and staring at some alien vista she could not imagine. At the same time she was aware that Vikas was gently ushering the children down the stairs, and the Lambas were coming up to look. She started to say, "He's sick, poor man, I'll get the doctor," for the sake of the children, but the boy Ajeet interrupted her.

"He's dead," he said scornfully. He gave her a defiant half grin. "I kicked his foot, so I know."

At the precise moment before the Lambas reached the landing, Divya saw two things: the piece of paper in the dead man's hand and the blue vial of rat poison standing quite close to his ragged pillow. In that instant she had swooped down and gathered both items, covering them with the pallu of her sari. She turned to face the Lambas. Mrs. Lamba gave a high-pitched cry and fell against her husband, who, not being built to handle the weight, tottered against the wall. Mrs. Bhosle took over, muttering words of comfort and calling for brandy, giving Divya an unexpectedly sympathetic look. Mr. Lamba drew himself up to his full height. Divya noticed that the tip of his nose was quite pale.

"What is the meaning of this! Who is this fellow?"

"The father-in-law of my neighbor's servant," Divya said. "They don't feed him—"

"I don't care who he is," Mr. Lamba said. "How can you tolerate having riff-raff living in your building? The man could be danger-ous! Or have a disease! Like AIDS!"

Mrs. Lamba shook herself loose from Mrs. Bhosle's grip. She pointed an accusing finger at Divya.

"What will I tell my sister when she gets back from London! Her son has been subjected to this . . . this unspeakable sight! The poor boy! And you call yourself a hostess! Wife of a vice president!"

She turned to the other guests standing in shocked silence on the steps.

"Let us leave this horrible place . . . these . . . people," she said. "They have no standards." She turned to Divya, shook a finger in her face. "Never have I been so insulted in all my life!"

Divya looked from the dead body of the man to the upturned faces. Mrs. Bhosle shook her head, but nobody said anything to contradict Mrs. Lamba.

"Yes, please leave," Divya said firmly. Charu had begun to sob against her father's chest. Poor Vikas—he looked completely shocked. Mrs. Bhosle and Mrs. Raman helped everyone find purses and shawls, and then ushered them all out. Divya did not say any goodbyes except to thank Mrs. Bhosle and Mrs. Raman for their help. Already, as the party was going down the stairs, she could hear Mrs. Chaturvedi's high, whining voice, eagerly discussing the incident. The ladies would feast off it for many parties and dinners to come.

While they waited for the police to arrive, Charu cried against her mother's shoulder, her sobs shaking her whole body. Divya could do nothing but hold her. Waves of guilt washed over her. If only she could go back to that moment when the old man had knocked on the door and Charu had been taking the parathas to him! Perhaps the parathas would not have saved him (the damned things were still in the fridge)—but who could tell? The poor man, to die like that! It wasn't fair—to raise your son and grow old, and be turned out to starve . . . Nor was it fair that she, Divya, was to be punished for one moment of carelessness, one instant where she had forgotten the right thing to do—and that this oversight should carry so much weight that it outweighed all her earlier acts of kindness to the old man, the giving of food, and the chance to earn a little money and respectability. Had none of that counted for anything? Would she now have to tiptoe through the world, watching for any lapse, any moment of forgetfulness? If the punishment was to be hers alone, she could bear it—but how cruel of the world, to punish a child instead: Charu in her new blue dress, who had learned on the day she turned twelve that Death lived in the world, and in time it would devour everyone she loved. And that it was possible to die alone and unloved. How does a child of twelve recover from that?

That moment . . . she kept returning to it in her mind. If only she hadn't been so hungry at the time! If Damyanti hadn't given Vikas those pakoras, or if Vikas hadn't been asking her about the rat poison . . .

The rat poison. A cold terror swept over Divya. How had the rat poison gotten to the old man's bedside?

She heard Vikas pacing to and fro in the drawing room, waiting for the police.

She had put the blue vial back on the bathroom shelf, behind the shampoo. The little square of stiff paper that had been in the dead man's hand she had put in the little dresser drawer where she kept her jewelry. It was a black and white picture—she hadn't had time to look at it properly. Now she made Charu sip some water.

"He was an old man, Charu," Divya said. "He was ill. Nothing we could have done would have saved him."

And so we lie to our children, she thought bitterly.

Charu choked on the water, coughed.

"He said the rats were running all over him at night . . ."

Divya held her breath. "Did you give him the rat poison?"

Charu nodded. "He said the rats were really big and he was afraid of getting bitten . . ."

Divya steadied herself, patted the child's hair.

"Listen, Charu, what you did was fine, but I don't want you to mention it to anyone. All right? Don't say anything about what the old man said or what you did. Let Papa and me talk to the policemen."

Charu's eyes went wide.

"Oh mama, do you think . . . oh, do you think . . ."

"No, no, child, quiet now. Everything is going to be fine."

Two policemen came, took notes, banged on the servant's door and on Mr. Kapadia's as well, but there was no answer. It was Saturday and Ranu and her husband were out—if Mr. Kapadia was in, he didn't care. The policemen didn't seem to care either. They nodded when Divya talked about how Ranu and her family had neglected the old man but shrugged when she asked if they would be brought to task.

"If we launched an investigation each time some old fellow dies of starvation, we would be overwhelmed," said one. They got up and left the family to the silence, the splendid ruins of the birthday party.

During a visit to the bathroom, Divya got a chance to look at the picture the old man had been holding when he died. It was a black-and-white photo, creased with age, and it was nearly impossible to make out whose picture it was. Divya would look at it many times in the next few months and wonder if the person was a woman or an animal or something entirely different.

Divya slept next to Charu that night, something she had not done in many years. They both slept fitfully. Divya felt sorry for

Vikas, tossing alone in the big bed in the next room. It would soon be time to worry about what would happen to his job. How strange that their fates should be tied to one old man whom nobody had known, whose speech nobody had understood. (Except for Charu—she realized, with a shock, that Charu must have been able to understand him to carry out his last request). Simply by dying, the old man would change their daughter's view of the world, and affect Vikas's career and the delicate network of social connections and links in which he existed, and change Divya herself in ways that she was yet to discover. She wondered what the old fellow had been trying to tell her these past years, in his broken voice; she should have listened more closely. She should have . . . she should have . . .

The old man lay in the center of her whirling thoughts like an enigma. Some of the tears she wept that night were for him, but as sleep slowly came to her she realized that she had never known his name.

*

In the weeks and months that followed, Vikas gave up his job, changed companies and began to plan a move to a different apartment in a different part of town. His new job was not as prestigious or as well-paying as the old one had been, and Divya could tell that he was unhappy. He began to play around with an old hobby, photography, disappearing for hours sometimes on weekends, and coming back to plunge himself in the darkroom he had set up in a storeroom in the flat. He refused to talk about the terrible incident, which bothered Divya because before this she had been able to talk to him about everything. Charu had the resilience of youth; she appeared to recover quite quickly, although her school performance suffered in the months following the incident. But Divya could tell that something had changed within the child. There was a sadness about her eyes that Divya could sense even when Charu was laughing with her friends. Charu had always been a softhearted girl, but after the incident she could no longer bear any kind of cruelty, nor could she, as a consequence, watch the news without tears. Divya worried how Charu would live in the world, whether she would learn to adapt enough to survive its horrors. She feared also that Charu blamed her for the whole thing, but apart from the inevitable distancing that growth brings, there was no indication of this. There were times when the girl would come upon her mother and give her a fierce, deep hug for no reason at all, and Divya felt Charu was trying to tell her something in some other language, and that she was able to comprehend it in that other language as well.

But the change in Divya herself was perhaps the most peculiar. She had, like most mothers, always been sensitive to the needs of those she loved, but now she was able to anticipate them even before there was any evidence of them. She knew, for instance, that Charu would have her period tomorrow and that the cramps would be bad; consequently she refused to let Charu go to school that day. She knew in the morning if Vikas was going to have a bad day at work, and when Kallu the crow landed on her kitchen window with an injured wing, she knew it before he had alighted.

When she went out, however, the gift or curse that had been left for her by the old man's death took its strangest form. When she looked upon the faces of strangers they appeared to her like aliens, like the open mouths of birds, crying their need. But most clearly she could sense those who were hungry, whether they were school children who had forgotten their lunch or beggars under the bridge, or the boot boy at the corner, or the emaciated girl sweeping the dusty street in front of the municipal building. Even in the great tide of humanity that thronged the pavements, amidst busy office goers and college students with cell phones, or in the shadows of the high-rises and luxury apartment blocks, she could sense the hungry and forgotten, great masses of them, living like cockroaches in the cracks and interstices of the new old city. Their open mouths, gaping and horrific with need, at first frightened her, but then she began to carry about with her a few parathas, which she handed out to the hungry without a word, in the hope that the keening chorus of despair that nobody but she was able to hear would lessen a little. Although this didn't happen, she found herself unable to stop handing out parathas to the needy. Meanwhile she continued to read her science fiction novels because, more than ever, they seemed to reflect her own realization of the utter strangeness of the world. Slowly the understanding came to her that these stories were trying to tell her a great truth in a very convoluted way, that they were all in some kind of code, designed to deceive the literary snob and waylay the careless reader. And that this great truth, which she would spend her life unraveling, was centered around the notion that you did not have to go to the stars to find aliens or to measure distances between people in light-years.

"A Source of Immense Richness"
Vandana Singh interviewed by Terry Bisson

Did you fall into SF or climb into it?
I fell into it, from a planet called the Third World.

Who are you?
I am an amalgam of recycled star cores and hydrogen, formed so that the universe could talk to itself. Just like you and that rock over there. In addition, I am a nonlinear combination of various apparent contradictions: earthling and alien, animal and tree, mammal and earthworm, to name a few.

What kind of car do you drive? (I am required to ask this of everyone.)
I've almost forgotten I have a car. Isn't that wonderful? I haven't driven it much during the pandemic. My steed is an aging Toyota.

Do you have a favorite city in the US? In India?
Not really. I have favorite places in cities, but cities as we currently conceptualize them are not my thing. There's a spacetime location in Delhi where/when I lived as a teen, with fruit trees and wild birds, clean air and blue skies, but it no longer exists. There

are a couple of cafés in Boston I like. And the Japanese Garden in Portland, Oregon.

Several of your stories feature food. Are you a good cook?
No, but I'm good at eating good food. I am a middling sort of cook with a limited repertoire, but I love good food across cuisines. I miss proper Indian cooking. I frequently wish someone would cook for me.

You grew up in a literary family. How did that come about?
A long family tradition that valued learning. I grew up in a vast family of grandparents, aunts, uncles, cousins, parents and siblings, and because there were no cell phones then and hardly anyone we knew had a TV, we read voraciously. We were not rich, but almost all the adults had college degrees. We didn't have much, but my parents had steel trunks filled with books on every subject under the sun, so I taught myself elementary German, memorized Greek myths, learned anatomical drawing, read writers well above my age level, and learned to immerse myself in the magic of story by the time I entered my teens. I also listened to accounts from elders on subjects as varied as ancient Indian poetry, the Ramayana, the relationships between languages, folk tales, the wretchedness of the caste system, and the fight for independence from British rule. So it was a rich intellectual atmosphere for a child to grow up in.

What do you like most about New England? Least?

I like the fact that no matter which way you throw a tennis ball, you're going to hit a university. The place is thick with them! What I don't like is the winter when it's being wimpy and not a real winter. We've been having too many of those lately. Rain in January!

What current controversies in physics do you find most interesting or intriguing?

The nature of dark matter and dark energy; why the universe's expansion is accelerating. Whether there are other universes than ours. What life as we don't know it—on other worlds and maybe our world—might be like. The nature of quantum information. The nature of time. Whether a unified theory exists or if the laws of the universe are more like a tapestry that shifts and shimmers as you examine it. The possibility of formulating theories with concepts and mathematics that don't exist as yet.

"The universe is much more like a hippie's pipe dream than it is like an accountant's ledger." Explain, please.

Ah, that's my ad for my modern physics course. After a hefty dose of Newtonian physics, in which we have a well-behaved, predictable universe, in which you can calculate the trajectory of a ball or the orbit of a planet with pretty good accuracy—after all this good behavior, we find ourselves in a strange place where the flow of time is affected by speed and gravity, particles may wink into or out of existence, light can be wavelike or particle-like, and you, the observer, become part of the experiment—well, that beats any drug-induced hallucination I've ever heard about, and it has no unpleasant side effects.

What writers have influenced you?
This is a very long list, so I'll just name a few. I grew up on the short stories of the great Hindi writer Premchand. From him I learned that a writer's empathic imagination can extend beyond their social stratum and gender. Because poetry and music are part of the air I breathed in Delhi (that was before the pollution) I also absorbed into my consciousness the ancient Sanskrit poets Kalidasa and Jayadeva, and medieval poets of my city, like Ghalib. Through them I discovered the power of metaphor. They reinforced that we lived with other species, that in their world clouds could be messengers, and that human love, despite being absurd, could stand for metaphysical union. There were the great epics, like the *Ramayana* and its multiple versions, from which I learned about the rhythm of story, and that the arc of plot could turn on one act by an unimportant character.

More recently and from this part of the world, I have been inspired and encouraged by Ursula K. Le Guin, who showed me that science fiction could be my country too, allowing me to take my first giddy steps into this strange land. I learned from Octavia Butler that hell is only a small spacetime interval away, always; and from all of them and more people than I can name in this small space, I learned to love this thing we call imaginative literature as (almost) the only hope we have.

You lived in Austin. To teach or study? Did you connect with the Austin music scene?

I lived in Austin as a young, married woman with a child, as part of a ten-year period of exile from academia, which I sorely missed. What I loved about the almost three years I spent in Austin was the time I got to spend with my small daughter, counting primroses in the park or playing with our dog, and learning how to see the world anew through a child's eyes. There were other not-so-nice things in the suburb of Austin where we lived, including some rather blatant racism, but I did get to be part of the music culture there—specifically the Indian music scene. There was a rather large population of people from India, and classical Indian music concerts used to be held regularly. We saw many great artists perform. I have a little training—only about three years—in North Indian classical vocal music, and I grew up in a musical family, so that meant a lot.

What music do you listen to most?

Depending on my mood, it could be North Indian classical, Bollywood oldies, reggae, classic rock, R&B, Western classical, jazz, or folk music from around the world.

Do you keep hours, habits, routines, or rituals as a writer?

Well, I have a very busy day job as a professor at a small university, so I don't get to write much during the semester. The only semiregular habit I have is to write about two or three times a week, even if it is only a paragraph, to keep the creative juices flowing. When summer comes I do this more regularly, and often the random little snippets become seeds for a story. I wish I could say I have mysterious rituals, like dancing to drumbeats by the light of the moon while waving a scimitar, but alas that would not be true.

What science writers do you read with pleasure?
I don't get to read much popular science, but I do read *Scientific American* and *New Scientist* as well as specific journal articles for research or curiosity.

Do you like American films? What about Bollywood? Are movies part of growing up in India?
I would like to be more literate in film. I haven't seen very many films, apart from a few classics. Bollywood is certainly an important part of growing up in India, but I was too much of a bookworm to care much about movies when I was growing up. And we didn't have a TV until my teens, which was too late for me to get habituated to the screen. But I have seen many, if not most of the Hindi classics, and I know a number of the songs. During my last winter break I started to explore Kurosawa. I do admire good movies—the medium is so different from writing, and therefore the aesthetics and imperatives are different too.

Ever spend time in the Himalayas?
Yes, from childhood visits to hill stations, to a life-changing trip in the summer between the end of high school and the beginning of

college, and my most recent visit in 2019. The life-changing visit at the age of seventeen was with a group of Delhi students to visit the Chipko movement, a now-famous ecofeminist movement of Himalayan villagers for forest rights and environment. Although this trip was decades ago, I remember details with vivid clarity;. It was one of those paradigm-shifting things that shake you loose from all previously held assumptions about the world. So while I fell in love with the Himalayas during my childhood, it was that visit as a teen that cemented a permanent relationship marked by a constant ache of longing when I am away. In 2019 I got to see a part of the range I had never visited before, in the Eastern Himalayas, and felt as though I belonged there as much as the bamboo and pine growing on the mountain slopes. Other people might be haunted by ghosts; I'm haunted by an entire mountain range.

In terms of reading and writing, what are the most interesting differences between Hindi and English?

Well, they are both Indo-European languages, so there are, first of all, similarities, for example in the roots of many words. Against this backdrop of deep-past common origin are some intriguing differences. In Hindi the verbs tend to be at the end of a sentence, and the script is far more precise than that of English—we have more letters, as a result. There are sounds in Hindi that don't exist in English. Also, while multiple literary styles abound in Hindi as well as English, it is easier to be emotional in Hindi than in English, to express passion without sounding purplish, although purplitude may also be embraced with abandon, as in the most unabashed Bollywood movies. As is true with comparing most languages, there are concepts that exist in Hindi that can't be translated into English. It is my mother tongue, so I find in it an indescribable sweetness; certain phrases evoke childhood memories, aromas, tastes of favorite foods, voices of people long gone.

Why are there so many different languages in India? Is that a feature or a bug?
It's definitely a feature. There are many cultural groups in India that have different histories, including linguistic histories. And apart from the officially recognized languages, of which there are over twenty, there are thousands of dialects. It's often hard to talk across these, which is why the colonial language, English, has such a hold still. There are plenty of quarrels across languages, but for me it is a source of immense richness to have so many languages and therefore so many different ways to see the world. Although I only know Hindi really well, I can sing in Bengali, and I used to be able to speak fairly good Tamil.

A sentence on each, please: Lee Smolin, Vandana Shiva, Molly Gloss.
Lee Smolin: you can trust him not to string you along. Vandana Shiva: I haven't followed her work lately, but a certain phrase of hers resonates: monoculture of the mind. Molly Gloss: Her writing is full of silences that speak—spare, passionate in the most understated way, evocative, and unforgettable.

Which of your children do you like best?
I only have one, so that's easy! She's my heart's joy.

Do you read poetry for pleasure? Who?
I grew up in a poetic culture, so it's as natural to me as breathing. Among Indian poets, I've already mentioned a few above, but there are also Sahir Ludhianvi, Dushyant Kumar, and Jacinta Kerketta. Among poets from other parts of the world, I love Neruda, Rumi, Hafez, Byron, Wordsworth, Keats, Angelou, Hikmat, Harjo, and so many others. I don't have any kind of deep knowledge of their works, but poetry is part of my basic four food groups.

My Jeopardy *item. I provide the answer: Keynes and Feynman. You provide the question.*
An economist and a physicist walk into a bar and discover that they are not at all keen on each other, although the beer is fine. Who are they?

How's your novel going?
It isn't! I don't have time to write anything that long, so my head is filled with larvae of novels, some in chrysalid sleep, others growing fat and impatient, and still others moribund.

The Room on the Roof

THE OLD WOMEN, THE grandmothers and widows in white saris, say that the monsoons awaken longings in all beings. The rain calls, they say, to hidden things, to seeds sleeping in the earth, to desire in the desiccated branches of trees and in the hearts of the young. As they tend the stove in the houses of their grown sons or daughters, as they sit on the balcony to sort rice or shell peas, as they look unseeingly at the grimy skyline of the city of their exile, they recount these myths and village lore, embroidered by their own imaginings and unfulfilled longings. Nobody listens but the young ones; the grown-ups, busy with jobs, chores and bank balances, have no time to draw from wells of wonder. News of a storytelling grandmother goes from house to house, and soon the audience swells to accommodate the children of neighbors.

The girl who watched from the window was one of these; not having grandparents of her own living with her (the two surviving ones lived in a remote village in Bengal), she had grown up with stories told by the grandmother of a friend on the next street. So her mind was open to the notion that behind the dreary ordinariness of the world were wonderfully strange impossibilities. Her name was Urmila and she had just turned thirteen.

It was the first rain of the monsoons. It had started with dark falling in the middle of the afternoon; then a mad wind had come down from the sky, banging doors and windows, making the washing flap crazily on clotheslines, driving before it the litter on the streets, blowing summer dust in clouds everywhere. When the rain came down in great, roaring, shining columns, there was a dash for shelter amid laughter and rejoicing, and dusty umbrellas blossomed. The children pulled free of scolding mothers and ran into the street to dance and shout. Only the girl Urmila and her nine-year-old brother, Somnath, stayed indoors, in the upstairs room they shared.

In past years Urmila too had celebrated the advent of the monsoons by dancing on the street with her friends; this year she felt a reluctance to do so. She waved at the yelling, gesticulating, laughing children below, and she smiled and shook her head, although there was a wistfulness about the way she perched on the damp sill, the way she cupped her chin in her dark, slender hand. Leaning on the metal grillwork of the window, she looked back at her brother, who was sprawled on his stomach on the other bed, his crutches flung carelessly on the floor. He was absorbed in a game of chess. The girl shivered suddenly and looked out again at the sky, the rain.

Over the steady, friendly sound of the rain Urmila was aware of other sounds: the movements of chess players over the board, her brother muttering, negotiating with an enemy knight, taking an enemy pawn by surprise. There was a beetle clattering about on the cold, bare floor of the room. Urmila's mathematics homework lay neglected and slightly damp on the desk near the window: a page full of carefully drawn Venn diagrams, circles intersecting circles, like so many overlapping universes. She had recently come to the conclusion that the world she lived in was not a separate, self-contained thing, but actually an intersection of many worlds. There was the world of the beetle, the world of her mother pounding spices in the kitchen downstairs, the chess-world, where her brother battled the evil enemy king, and who knows how many hidden worlds outside her awareness?

She was given to fanciful thoughts such as these, most of which she kept to herself out of embarrassment or shyness, but as she sat musing, looking out at the slowly drowning world, something extraordinary appeared at the end of the street.

It was a woman. She was walking down the street without an umbrella or a sense of urgency, looking about her, shading her eyes from the rain with one hand. Her bright green salwaar-kameez clung wetly to her skin as she splashed slowly through the water-logged street. The girl saw all this and a thought came into her mind: This is the woman who will change everything.

The woman paused at the girl's front gate, opened it and walked the few steps to the front door. The next moment a bell jangled in the house.

Later, when Urmila remembered the events of that rainy season, she wondered why she hadn't felt more surprised that the woman upon whom she had laid such a great responsibility—that of changing everything, or at least that one thing that had been worrying her—should have chosen, of all streets in Delhi, her particular street, and of all houses, this one house. Of course they had the room on the roof to rent, and an advertisement in the local paper, and they weren't more than a twenty-minute bus ride from the Vishwakarma Institute of Fine Arts, so you could explain the whole thing quite logically. But it was still quite extraordinary how it turned out . . .

At first, nothing much changed after the woman moved into the room on the roof. Her name was Aparna Bhuvan, and she was a sculptress; she brought with her just one suitcase, several lumps of clay and a faint fragrance of wet earth. She went every morning to the institute and returned in the evening with clockwork regularity. Urmila's mother approved of her because she was polite and decent, ate all her meals out and never brought anyone home. She was only a small ripple in the melancholy orderliness, the dull routine of the household, but to Urmila, she was a presence redolent with significance. The room on the roof was another world that had nothing to do with the rest of the house: the drawing room with its decades-old furniture, its display shelves crowded with bric-a-brac, the mute sitar propped in the corner; the neat parental bedroom with the mauve and brown sheets, the venerable sewing machine and gargantuan steel cupboards that smelled of mothballs and old dreams when they were opened. No, Aparna Bhuvan lived in a different world, Urmila imagined, one with earth-smells and rain-smells, colors and carefree untidiness. The woman herself was quiet and unobtrusive, but her brown eyes were alight with laughter and secrets, and her hair was always loose, resting on her shoulders like a cloud on a mountaintop. Her clothes were colored like rainbows, in swirls of red and ochre, or green and mustard-yellow. Every evening she would pass the children's room as she went light-footed up the stairs, and when she saw one of them looking out at her she would smile.

It rained without respite on most days, and dark fell early. In the evenings Urmila stayed in her room, reading and watching over her brother as he played his interminable games of chess with an invisible enemy. It had long ceased to be merely a game; last year, Som had cut a giant chessboard out of a piece of cardboard, marked the squares and then proceeded to put in the other features: the fort walls, the river, secret passages. The board was alive with mysterious symbols in black ink. The rules, too, had changed: the movements of the chessmen (each of whom had a name) were governed as much by intrigues, secret loyalties and betrayals, past histories, future aspirations—as by the traditional rules of chess. Urmila remembered how voluble and eager he had been last year, describing it all to her, building his world brick by brick. In this world the boy who could not play cricket or even walk without his crutches became a tall, turbaned warrior, fearless and compassionate. In her mind's eye she had seen him walk the passageways of the fort, inspecting the defenses, encouraging the men at the narrow slit-windows on the ramparts. His short brown fingers had lingered over a knight or pawn, his eyes seeing not the chessboard but the hills and valleys and townships of his embattled country.

But now he had shut her out with his silence. For months he had been reticent about his made-world, responding to Urmila's questions with a mulish sticking-out of his lower lip, or a shrug or a grunt, not meeting her eye, turning away from her as he had not done in all the years of his life. He had always been quiet, wary with strangers, set apart from his schoolmates by disability and temperament, but he had never been distant from her before. She was haunted by the growing certainty that one day he would disappear completely into the chess world, leaving nothing behind but a pair of crutches—and that this silence between them was the first phase of his retreat. There was nobody she could confide in. Her one close friend was out of town for the holidays. Her parents constantly fretted about Som's prospects—who would marry a cripple? How would he manage after they were gone? But now, as long as he did well in school and was healthy, they saw no reason to worry about him. Once Urmila had talked to her mother about Som, and her mother had said, "He will be a chess champion one day, like Kartik Krishnan." And she had wiped her eye with the corner of her sari and sighed.

When the sculptress had wrought no magic in her first week of tenantship, Urmila began to lose hope. One evening, after the dinner dishes had been cleared away, and her father had established himself on the sofa with the newspaper, Urmila went up to him.

"Papa?"

She had rehearsed it all in her head: Som's retreat into the chess-world, his silence, his turning away from her. But her father said, in his soft, deep voice, "Turn on the TV, child. It's time for the news."

The words died on her tongue. She did as she was told and stood leaning against the doorway. The TV man's prophet-of-doom voice filled the room: the gross national product had fallen again and the Northeast crisis had taken a turn for the worse. Urmila's mother came in and sat down on the sofa, stirring isabgol into a glass of water with a spoon, a nightly ritual to ward off constipation. The sofa dipped and creaked with her weight. Her husband glanced at her in irritation and she stopped stirring and began to drink, talking between gulps in her tentative, Bengali-accented Hindi about her day, the rise in the price of flour, the servant-maid's tardiness. "Quiet!" snapped Urmila's father, leaning forward into the TV's glare. "This is important . . ."

If Aparna Bhuvan had truly possessed magic, Urmila thought, the TV would have blinked out with a wave of the hand. And then the sitar in the corner, the sitar her father had studied and given up when his father died, would have spoken; the strings would stir, softly at first, and then the music would fill the room. As her parents looked around in wonder (she imagined) the souvenirs on the shelves (gifted by globetrotting friends and relatives) would come alive: the little dancing girl from the mountains of Assam would begin to smile and sway, the windmill from the Netherlands would start turning its great wheel . . . Urmila let out a deep breath and left the room.

Now even her room, which had been a refuge of sorts from the rest of the house, began to oppress her, with the moist patch on the ceiling and the square window framing incessantly falling rain.

"This terrible rain," Urmila's mother would say, oiling Urmila's hair, combing it out in long, slow strokes. "Your red kurta took three days to dry on the verandah—three days! I told Dhanu to iron it for you but she has left early again, the lazy girl . . ."

Every week Urmila braved the murky weather to go to Charu's house on the next street, where Charu's grandmother held court. From the open windows came the endless pattering of rain and odorous gusts of wind from the swollen river. The children waited restlessly for the stories, munching crisp, spicy hot pakoras, wiping oily hands unconsciously on their clothes. The grandmother's stories matched the mood of the season: they were delightfully scary tales of ghosts in banyan trees and things that came out of wells. "Dead things," the grandmother would say, "rocks and dust and bones, all desire life. Their hunger is so great that it brings the monsoons to us, so that they may, at least for a while, know what it is to be alive. And the fire-fiend comes out of the marshes, and disturbs the village girls . . ."

But nothing ever happens here, thought Urmila.

One evening after dinner, after her brother had retreated upstairs, Urmila went to help in the kitchen—the servant-maid had been unable to come. When her parents were huddled together before the TV, listening to the news with the blind innocence of grown-ups, she made her way slowly up the dark stairway. Light spilled from the open door of her room, and the bass cackle of the TV retreated with every step. Her eyes filled suddenly with tears.

But her room was empty. She looked up the stairs to the light from another doorway, from which she heard the soft murmur of conversation punctuated with laughter. She stood on the landing for a long time, caught between the two worlds, above and below. Then she went into her room, found a book and gazed unseeingly at it until her brother returned. She did not look at him. When he turned out the light a little later, she heard the familiar creak of his bed and a small sigh against the wall.

After that Som went up to see the sculptress nearly every evening. Once Urmila crept up the stairs and crouched on the fifth step from the top. Her brother was standing leaning against the part-open door, silhouetted against the light from within, his crutch held idly under one arm. She could just see Aparna Bhuvan's brown, skilled hands shaping a moist lump of clay on the table with sinuous, graceful movements. Every once in a while her face would come into view, with the humorous, mobile mouth, the eyes agleam in the light, a strand of black hair falling across her clay-streaked cheek. The window in the room must have been open because the air smelled cool and moist, and the clamor of the rain filled the ears of the watching, listening girl.

They were talking about the chess world.

"A good strategist concentrates on what he can change." The sculptress's hands paused at their work while she spoke as seriously as if she were talking about events in the real world. The sound of the rain rose to a crescendo and then faded. "The king, now, he cannot change everything. Of course," now a smile crept into her voice, "he has to find out first, what it is he can change, and what he can't."

The boy said something inaudible and they both laughed.

The next afternoon, when the sculptress passed the children's room on her way upstairs, she smiled at them both as usual but her eyes lingered in a kindly way on Urmila. So Urmila knew that Aparna Bhuvan had been aware of her watching and listening the night before. After that she stayed in her room in the evenings.

Then one day she noticed a small clay soldier on her brother's desk. It was unpainted, an earthy orange-red, so real that it startled her. The end of the soldier's turban flapped behind him in a permanent breeze; one hand shaded his eyes from the sun, and in the other he held a spear. When (in her brother's absence) she touched the figure with a tentative finger, it felt almost warm, as though it had only lately emerged from the kiln.

After that she began to notice a difference in her brother. Som still didn't talk to her—he would lie on his bed, staring at the giant chessboard, glancing up to look at the soldier on his desk, swinging his crippled leg rhythmically over the edge of the bed as he planned the next move—but there was a lightness about him now, as though his center of gravity had mysteriously shifted. He seemed to lean more easily on his crutches; his shoulders no longer hunched defensively against the world. Urmila began to sense that the mysterious and troubling barrier between them was dissolving, and that she was being forgiven for some lapse, some insensitivity of word or deed that she had been trying to remember for a year.

But what finally turned hope to certainty was the object that she discovered on her desk one evening. It was a terra-cotta figurine of a young woman standing with her arms outstretched before her, in a gesture of greeting or release. Her long skirt swirled about her in a gust of intangible wind, and her hair streamed out behind like a banner.

Urmila stared; she picked up the little figure and turned it slowly in her hands.

"It's for you, Didi," her brother said. He looked hopefully at her. She took a deep breath, feeling light-headed with relief and delight. They smiled tentatively at each other.

"Aparna-di made it, she says will you come up and see her in the evenings?"

So Urmila came to understand that there was magic in the world, even if it worked at its own pace, in its own way. Certainly there was something magical about the room on the roof: here the rain was no longer dismal—it sang to them, sometimes loud and wild, sometimes a lullaby. A fine spray often blew into the room from the open window, but no mold grew on the walls as it did in the other rooms. The light in here was warm and yellow, the air smelled earthy and wonderful, and the sagging bed was the most comfortable thing to sprawl on while the children watched the clay take shape under Aparna's hands. They would try to guess what each lump was destined to become and laugh at each other's guesses. The sculptress would laugh at them both.

"I never know what shape the clay will take," she'd say. "Clay has dreams too. When I mix earth with water, I feel the clay move under my hands; all I do is guide it."

"You must be the best sculptress in the world," Som said, once, eyes wide. She shook her head, smiling.

"I'm only a junior instructor at the institute. You should see some of the really good people at work."

She showed them the institute's yearbook; they leafed through glossy photos of paintings, sculptures in clay, stone and metal, vast studios filled with sunlight. So this was her other world. Here was a picture of her, in one of those sunny rooms, bending over a student's work. Now a full-page photograph of a man caught their attention: tall, slender, with round fanatical eyes under shaggy black eyebrows, his longish graying hair combed back like one of the more flamboyant movie stars. "Ah, the genius," Aparna said, glancing up from her work. Her tone was curiously flat. The nationally recognized artist, Vardhaman Mitra, the article said, in his beautiful home, surrounded by his work. His sculptures were abstract, fluid, suggestive.

"That's his wife, Renuka." Aparna pointed with a grimy finger at the picture of a smiling, statuesque woman in a glittering sari standing at the top of a marble staircase. "My friend. She used to be a sculptress too, a good one."

"Why doesn't she sculpt anymore?" Som lifted curious eyes from the page.

"Because she's forgotten who she is," the sculptress said harshly, turning away, slapping water on to the clay with unnecessary violence. "Now she is content to inspire him, or so she tells me."

"What's he like?"

She was quiet for a second or two.

"Vardhaman? Difficult," she said. "Ambitious. Arrogant."

It was some time before she smiled again.

The children finished looking through the yearbook and as Urmila closed it and set it on the bed beside them, she had the disturbing realization that the sculptress inhabited, for the better part of the day, a world completely unfamiliar to them, centered around Vardhaman Mitra and his glittering wife—a world of mysterious adult tensions, with no place for Urmila or her brother.

Their collection of her work grew. On Urmila's desk was an eagle, a dolphin and a creature that was half-bird, half-woman. For Som there was a long boat complete with tiny men bearing oars, a rectangular vase for his pencils and, incongruously, a life-size pair of clay shoes. They were amusing, those shoes, with their floppy laces, the frayed cuffs, the well-worn shape. For a boy who had to use crutches and wear special shoes this would have been a cruel gift from anyone else, mocking his deformity, but from Aparna Bhuvan it was a happy, amusing present.

About this time Urmila began to have vivid dreams that were sometimes disturbing in their intensity. In these dreams she knelt in pools of wet clay, her hands cupped, pouring the silken, liquid mud onto her legs and arms. Snakes rose from the clay pools and slid into the undergrowth with sinuous grace, and once a bird emerged, wet and earth-colored, and took flight. Always, the sculptress was a subtle presence in her dreams, no more tangible than a shape in the distance, an awareness behind the trees. Sometimes she dreamed of her brother; lately it had been the same dream: the rain had stopped and moonlight came through the window, falling on the bare floor in a wash of silver light. Som was dancing in the middle of the room without his crutches, his clay shoes making a comical, hollow sound as he turned and dipped and whirled. When she woke and sat up in bed after one of these dreams, the moonlight was real, but her brother was fast asleep in his bed, in the dark shadows at the far end of the room. In the rainless stillness his breathing seemed to fill the space between them. She lay back, lulled to sleep by the rise and fall of his breath.

The next evening, as she watched Aparna at work, Urmila found herself wondering about her. The sculptress liked to talk as she worked but she never spoke about herself, the way ordinary people did.

"Tell us about yourself," Urmila said abruptly. She wished she could be more graceful in her speech, but lately her words emerged without warning in awkward, staccato bursts. The sculptress looked startled for a moment. "Tell us—tell us about your home—where you come from. How you came here."

"I come from rather far away—a place where nothing ever happens. The kind of place you leave to see the world . . ."

"Is it as far away as Bengal?" Som said. "My nana and nani live there, in a village by the sea. We've only been once."

Urmila looked at him, surprised. He had been so little on that visit—was it possible he remembered?

"My mother never goes back home," he continued. "She's Bengali, you know, but my father isn't. They married . . . for love," he said shyly.

"We saw the sea only once," Urmila said. "But my father couldn't speak Bengali. He didn't like it. And he doesn't like fish. And my mother was supposed to marry someone else who still lives there. So we don't go there anymore."

She paused, thinking about the trip. Som said,

"We're talking about ourselves again. Tell us about your family, Aparna-di. And how you came to Delhi."

Her strong hands worked vigorously for a second or two. She picked up a round-tipped wooden tool and began to shape the clay. She looked at them through the hair falling over her face.

"Nothing much to tell. I grew up with Renuka, the lady you saw in the yearbook. We were closer than sisters. Then almost exactly two years ago she got the fever to see the world. She came here, joined the art institute. Never came back, only kept entreating me to join her. I've seen some of her early work—she could make the clay sing! But by the time I got here she was married and no longer working. I stayed with them for a while, then I wanted my own place. And here I am . . ."

She was speaking lightly, but her eyes were careful. Behind them lurked some unidentifiable emotion, Urmila thought, feeling her own eyes fill unexpectedly with tears, feeling shut out, stupid, ashamed.

"You'll stay here now, won't you?" Som said.

Aparna smiled ruefully.

"I'll go home someday, maybe sooner than I thought at first," she said. Urmila gripped the edge of the bed. "One must always go home, you know. It's like music. You start with a theme. You wander from it, using a raga or mode as your guide and constraint. You play around, but at the end you come back to the beginning. The beginning is the end."

"If you never go home," the sculptress said, bending over the clay, her hair a monsoon cloud on her shoulders, "you are like a kite whose string has been severed . . ."

Urmila thought of the sitar in the drawing room, and the village by the sea. Perhaps there was no magic, she thought with a pang. If the sculptress also knew pain in her life, if there were things she could not fix, why, she too was as human and helpless as any of them. There was nothing anyone could do. Then the rain started up again; Aparna began to sing as she worked, and Urmila's sudden gloom lifted as quickly as it had come.

As the rain-filled days passed Urmila was aware of a subtle change in herself. She had always thought of herself as quiet and steady, the kind of person people rely on to be responsible and stable, but now she was aware that there was a wildness in her, as though something inside was responding to the rain. She was filled with a desire to run out into the street, to fly up in the clouds. The world itself seemed more interesting and mysterious than it ever had before; it was rife with secrets, a place where so many other worlds intersected, and she wanted to discover and explore everything. In the circle of children that attended the grandmother's storytelling sessions every week she was gregarious, happy, and not at all shy. But sometimes a hopeless melancholy possessed her, and she thought the rain would never end, and that she and her brother and parents would never be happy or free, that beyond one wall there were others, an infinite concentricity of walls. Up in Aparna's room every evening, she felt joy and yearning like a fever, and underneath it the fear that all she had gained was temporary, that one day the sculptress would leave them and the magic would go out of their lives. Sometimes she caught herself holding her breath, waiting for the change.

But the change that came was not the tender, sorrowful parting she had been dreading. One evening Urmila was waiting for Aparna on the landing. It seemed to her that the sculptress was later than usual, and her brother too got to his feet on one crutch and limped over to join her. As they stood together, leaning against the banister in the semidarkness, with the TV going on below them, they saw Aparna coming in at last. Her hair was more disheveled than usual and her face was terrible and grim. Her eyes were like hot coals, furious, red-rimmed, bleak. She did not look at them. She ran past them up to her sanctum; they heard the door slam. The air around them still quivered with the swiftness of her passing, and there was the faint, familiar smell of moist clay.

Urmila put out an arm to steady Som, whose frightened breathing filled the darkness. She led him into the room and sat with him on his bed, putting an arm around him as she used to when he was younger.

She did not know how long they sat waiting, but the sculptress did not appear at their door. After a while she got up. "I'll be back," she said. She went like a ghost up the stairway. The door was shut. From within came the sounds of things breaking: baked clay statues shattering against the wall, unfinished clay thudding wetly on the floor. And guttural curses in an unfamiliar language, punctuated by howls of anguish. She imagined the sculptress whirling around the room in a dance of destruction, her hair whipping about her face, her eyes pouring forth tears of rage and loss. Urmila had never felt more a child, useless, helpless, shut out by mysterious storms in grown-up lives. She crept back down the stairs, trembling, uncertain what to tell Som, but he was standing at their door, looking up at her, listening. He had been crying. She blinked hard and took his arm, but they did not go into their room. It was all they had to offer, their silent, unacknowledged presence on the landing. They stood there until the sounds from above ceased and a dreadful silence took its place.

For three days the children stayed in their room in the evenings. They did their holiday reading, talked quietly to each other and did not speak of what had happened. But each glanced at the open door of the room when Aparna passed by on her way up.

Then one morning Urmila was sent to the milk booth, the servant maid having been taken sick. Walking away from the booth with the steel container cold and heavy in her arms, she looked towards the noisy main road. Beyond it lay the sodden cricket field and then the river, and on the other side, the specters of tall, grimy buildings, all boundaries smudged in the haze of slow rain. And there, in the park by the river, stood Aparna Bhuvan. Urmila watched, squinting in the rain. Then she trudged home.

The next evening the children heard voices at the bottom of the stairs. Urmila went to the door of their room. Downstairs her mother was holding a large fold of newsprint before her, talking to the sculptress. She pointed to something in the paper. Over the murmurs from the TV, Urmila heard Aparna say, "Yes, that's her . . . Yes, from my hometown."

"So very sad," said her mother.

There were more words exchanged that Urmila could not catch. Her mother's tone was curious, wistful, as though she wanted to continue the conversation, but at last she went back into the drawing room. Urmila watched Aparna come up the stairs; at the landing the sculptress looked at her with bright, sorrowing eyes, paused, and reached out one hand as though to touch Urmila's cheek. Urmila stood very still and stiff, and Aparna turned and continued up the stairs.

In the drawing room the TV was going on about unrest in the Northeast. Her mother was shaking her head, muttering to her husband.

". . . a fall, from a balcony. Vardhaman Mitra was away, the servants at the other end of the house . . . broke her neck . . ."

"Hmm . . ." said Urmila's father, leaning forward into the TV's glare.

". . . imagine what a shock I got, the same Mrs. Mitra who sent us that nice reference letter. What a tragedy!"

"Shh . . . I am trying to listen, for God's sake . . ."

Urmila picked up the newspaper from its basket near the door. Up in their room they spread it out on her bed. It took them some time to find the article. It was in the obituary pages. There was a picture of the deceased, the same one they had seen in the yearbook.

The sculptress's door was open. She was working on something; she looked up at them and at the newspaper, then she sighed and smiled all at once, and made a gathering gesture with one arm. They went in and sat on the bed, glancing around as though they had never been in the room before. She had cleaned up, but there were still faint marks on the walls. It had stopped raining—a moist breeze blew in through the window, but the street below was full of watery sounds, the splash of cars passing, the plink of pebbles thrown in a ditch by anonymous children. On the table there were two new pieces: a woman dancing, holding a two-headed drum, her skirt billowing out around her legs, and a boy with a kite in his arms, looking up at an imaginary sky. "For you," Aparna said, handing the figurines to the children, her eyes bright, tender, sorrowful. They held the gifts with careful, reverent fingers. Urmila wished she had a gift for Aparna that would ease her pain, but she felt crushed by the magnitude of the loss, and her own poverty.

"We've never given you anything," she said.

"Never say that," said the sculptress. She indicated the lump of clay on which she was working. "Can you guess what this is going to be?"

They watched as the clay began to transform under her fingers.

"It's a hand!" Som said after a while. "Two hands!"

Two hands with the fingertips pointing upwards, the palms facing each other. The wrists were slender, the fingers frozen in an exquisite mudra. A dancer's hands.

"Your hands . . . ?" Urmila said.

"This is my last piece," the sculptress muttered, as though to herself. "Everything I have made has been a gift. Thus I keep a promise, repay a debt . . ."

They looked uncomprehendingly at her, and after a while she looked up from her work.

"I'm going away," she said at last. The words hung in the air, and Urmila heard them echo slowly in her mind. "Home," said the sculptress, smiling sadly and tenderly at them. "I've given notice to your mother. It will be about a week I think."

They could find nothing to say. This was the moment Urmila had been waiting for, but nothing had prepared her for it. It seemed to her that everything had suddenly slowed: the sounds in the street below, the drip-drip of the rain from the roof of the house, the beating of her heart. Through a numbness that was spreading rapidly through her, she heard Som say something, and Aparna replied, shaking hair out of her face. Urmila looked quickly at him; he was quite composed, but she thought he would cry later, his face turned to the wall by his bed. A lump formed in her throat then, and she felt a great stirring of blind emotion, hot as lava, surging inside her.

She knew without asking that when the sculptress left there would be no forwarding address, no letters exchanged. The room would be empty, as it had been before. But the world would have changed. She wasn't sure how she would live in it.

Aparna began to clear out her room. She took her last sculpture to the desiccator and kiln at the institute, as usual, but she did not bring back the finished work. She packed her few clothes and sundry belongings away in her suitcase. For Urmila time seemed to pass quickly and confusingly; she could not keep up with it. Her chest felt full of butterflies.

Two days before Aparna left, the news came. It was in newspapers, on TV, in glossy magazines: the terrible, violent demise of Vardhaman Mitra. He had been found in his marble bedroom by the servants, strangled to death by an unknown assailant. The guard at the gate had heard nothing, nor had the servant polishing the banisters a few feet from the bedroom door. There had been no visitors, suspicious or otherwise. The newspaper had a picture of the great artist after his wife's death, looking shrunken, with desperate, hungry eyes. "I cannot work," he had said then. "She gifted me her dreams. I gave them shape in clay . . ." Now he too was dead, and his murderer had left no clues apart from the indentation of fingers around the neck of the corpse. There was no sign of a struggle, but for a clay sculpture that lay smashed beyond recognition on the floor.

Aparna did not comment on the tragedy. She answered Urmila's mother's questions willingly enough, shaking her head sorrowfully, nodding at all the right places. She went out to the dhobi's stand on the next street with the bedclothes and curtains and had them washed and ironed. It seemed as though she had already washed her hands of the affairs of the institute, that her mind was on the journey home.

Finally there came the evening of the last day. The sculptress had sent her suitcase on already. The table was clean and unfamiliar, the sheets on the bed smelled like the coal iron of the dhobi. It was raining again in a slow, sulky way, perhaps the last rain of the monsoon. Aparna Bhuvan was wearing her red-and-ochre salwaar-kameez, defying the grayness outside. Around her neck was a silver necklace Urmila had given her (a gift from some forgotten relative when Urmila had been small), and in her hand she held Som's queen from the chess set. She thanked them with bright eyes.

Urmila said, "Are you taking the train?" and did not understand when Som and Aparna both laughed gently at her. Of course, she would take the bus first, Urmila thought. Her mind felt thick. Aparna embraced first Urmila, then Som, enveloping them briefly in the fragrance of moist earth. Now she was making her way down the stairs, Som following, thumping on his crutches. The boy and the sculptress said something to each other at the landing, then he went into the room and she continued down the stairs, getting smaller and smaller, like a bucket being let down into a well. She paused at the door to the drawing room, limned for a moment in the garish light from the TV, and said something to Urmila's parents. Then she was gone.

The sound of the front door shutting woke Urmila from her stupor; she began to run down the stairs, two at a time. Som called out to her but she didn't stop. The streetlight outside the house was out but she saw Aparna several paces ahead, walking quickly and gracefully through puddles and over potholes. The narrow street was lined with cars, and the rain cascaded gently off them. Urmila followed quickly, not knowing what compelled her, or what she would tell Aparna when she caught up with her. On the main road, with the crowds, the cacophony of car horns and the glare of headlights, she lost her quarry for a moment and stood looking frantically about, soaked to the skin, her hand shading her eyes from the rain. A man nudged up against her, leering, and she gave him a fierce, indignant look and joined a group of people with umbrellas crossing the street to the bus stop on the other side. But Aparna was not there. Urmila looked behind the bus stop at the soggy cricket field, and the dark river beyond it, and the wavering city lights on the other side. There she was, standing on the riverbank, staring away at something. What was she doing there? There was a bus coming now, it would go most of the way to the railway station. People dropped off the bus as it lurched, belching, to a stop; now the crowd surged towards it in a body. Urmila slipped away into the darkness behind the bus stop and plunged ankle-deep into the mud of the cricket field.

The sculptress was standing, stretching her arms before her, bending her body as if in obeisance to the rain. She lifted her face and let the rain fall on it. Only a faint wash of light from the street fell on her; she was a dark silhouette against the murky, glimmering river. Urmila stumbled towards her, dragging one foot, then another in the mud. Aparna must surely have seen her by now, she paused in her stretching and swaying, and perhaps she smiled. Urmila stopped. Aparna knelt, rain falling on her in thick shawls. Now Urmila saw that she was naked, except for the gleam of the silver necklace around her neck; somehow her clothes had rolled off her, or had been dissolved in the rain. She was holding something—the chess queen?—in one hand. Rain fell on her bare shoulders, formed a thick rivulet between her breasts, cascaded over the dimple in her belly, pooled in the hollow below, flowed smoothly over her thighs. Her hands dug into the mud; she bent her head, her hair falling in a wet, tangled mass over her face. Now a forest of hands rose from the mud, clay hands, loving hands, drawing the woman down into the earth. Her body seemed to become molten; a ripple ran over her. Before she sank completely, before her shape had altogether lost form, she raised her head and looked at the girl standing in the rain. Then there was nothing there but trampled mud, and the rain falling on it, smoothing it.

Urmila felt it then: a lightness spreading inside her, not joy, not pain, but something more complex, a kind of effervescence. She began to walk home in the rain. On her street the house lights shone warmly; open windows let out the sounds of conversation, laughter, plates in the sink. In Charu's house the grandmother would be tucking the smallest ones into bed, telling them a story about the monsoons. Urmila understood at last that what the monsoons brought was nothing less than the possibility of dissolving barriers between worlds.

Inside her gate she paused. She could hear the babbling of the TV; the blue light flickered in the window. She stood in the rain, feeling reluctant to go in. It fell on her like a benediction. Over the sound of the rain, the cackle of the TV, she heard it, so soft and tentative that she must have imagined it: the hollow clunk of clay shoes on the floor of the room upstairs, dancing, dancing to the rain.

True Journey Is Return: A Tribute to Ursula K. Le Guin

IT IS DIFFICULT TO put into words what I am feeling at the death of a great writer and a great human being. That Ursula K. Le Guin happened to have taken an interest in me and my work is part of why my grief is personal, but not entirely. She was a generous human being and a kind mentor who took interest in the works of multiple authors, so my story of our association is, I am sure, not unique, except, perhaps, in the particularities of the interaction. We met three times—once for six days during a writing retreat—and corresponded a couple of times a year on average. But in my life she had a disproportionate effect, and it is safe to say that I would not be the writer or the person I am without the deep and abiding influence of who she was and what she wrote. So what follows is an account made somewhat incoherent by the aftershocks of grief, for which I apologize in advance.

In the great six-book saga of *Earthsea*, which is to modern fantasy what, perhaps, the Mahabharata is to epic literature, there are many gifts for the reader. One of them is the landscape—so beautifully detailed in words and maps that it lives as vividly in my imagination as the great epics I first heard as a child. Another is that most of the characters in the books are brown—not in any overt way, but because it is, well, normal in that world. That representation matters can hardly be overstated—I am thinking of Nichelle Nichols, Lieutenant Uhura of *Star Trek: The Original Series*, and how she inspired generations of African Americans to take up science and the pen. But unlike *Star Trek*, Le Guin went beyond tokenism to present genuinely different perspectives arising from different cultural moorings. Her upbringing as the daughter of one of America's most famous anthropologists, Alfred Kroeber (an experience she recounts in fascinating detail in her essay collections), enabled her to be aware of the multiple ways different social groups structure themselves and their worlds. Eventually she was instrumental in bringing down the walls around the almost exclusively male, boys-with-toys shoot-'em-up club that was golden-age science fiction.

I didn't discover her through the *Earthsea* series, however. I came to her work late, in my early thirties. I had always loved SF, having devoured, by the age of ten or eleven, Asimov, Clarke, a number of Hindi tall tales and some truly awful Tom Swift novels. Later, there was Bradbury's *Fahrenheit 451*, which showed me that science fiction could be literature. But in my late teens I abandoned the genre for reasons that remained unclear to me for years.

My brother had been insisting for some years that I read a book called *The Dispossessed* by Ursula K. Le Guin. When I finally picked it up, I was a mother in my early thirties, living near Portland, Oregon, trying my hand for the first time at writing with a view to publication. I had always told stories, thanks to the vociferous demands of my younger sister when she was little, a skill I had already started practicing for my daughter. Science fiction seemed a natural fit for someone with a physics PhD, so I had returned to the genre, although with some trepidation. When I closed *The Dispossessed* with what must have been shaking fingers, a new universe lay open before me, and I was overcome by feelings I could not articulate. Soon after, I read the first three books of the *Earthsea* series. It gradually became clear to me that what I was feeling was a homecoming—that science fiction was my country too. That the futures, trajectories, and philosophies imagined in the books of Asimov, for example, were not the only choices at hand. The possibilities were endless—not merely in terms of external markers like skin color but in alternate ways of being, social relationships, worldviews. Here was the true revolutionary potential of imaginative fiction.

I was born in a free India, but the country was only fifteen years free when I was born. I had the benefit of being raised in a family with an open intellectual tradition; I had relatives who had been freedom fighters, and my grandparents, parents, aunts, and uncles encouraged us to ask questions and seek learning. I had grown up reading great Hindi writers like Premchand, who questioned social norms like caste and class. Later, in my teens I was part of an environmental justice action group in India that helped me see firsthand how the lives of the rural poor were intimately connected to the environment and to state and social violence. In this context we were able to question the dominant paradigm of development. But I first became *conscious* of the need to decolonize that last frontier—the mind—while journeying through the worlds of Ursula Le Guin's imagination.

I tell this story because I want to emphasize that Le Guin, by presenting worldviews, and indeed worlds, as constructs, provincialized the default Western traditions as merely one of many possibilities. Other writers had been dreaming up other planets and gadgets and gizmos since the birth of SF. But the heroes were for the most part, white and male, and they thought in ways that reflected the birth culture of their writers. Westerns in space. The language and plot lines of colonization. Even writers sympathetic to the fate of the colonized—I'm thinking of Ray Bradbury's beautiful *Martian Chronicles*, a meditation on colonization—rendered their alien wives as one-dimensional servers of dinner and emotional support. What Le Guin did was to take down the walls around the imagination, and to set us all free. To shift the paradigms, the conceptual constructs by which we make sense of the world, is no small thing.

Soon after reading Le Guin, I had a chance to meet her at a writers' conference in Portland. There was a mini writers' workshop, conducted by her, Molly Gloss, and Tony Wolk. She turned out to be a small, sprightly woman with an intensely intelligent, yet kindly gaze, and a rapier-sharp wit. Waving away our fannish adulations, she insisted we call her Ursula. After the workshop she encouraged me to write to her, and to apply to a writers' retreat, Flight of the Mind, in the Oregon forest. She thought a writers' critique group would help me, and Molly said she would introduce me to a friend of hers. So began my first writers' group, and my journey as a writer.

I did go to Flight of the Mind in 1999, after we had moved away from Oregon. Six days with some sixty women, in the middle of the great temperate rainforests of Oregon, was an unforgettable experience. I was one of twelve who had signed up with Ursula—we would walk across a bridge over the river to Ursula's cottage, sit on the floor in a circle, and talk, and do writing. Gradually our awe at being in her presence gave way to ease. There was a lot of laughter. We wrote, critiqued, went for walks through the woods, and ate vast quantities of food. My memories of the time are filled with the sound of the river (a constant backdrop to our conversations) and an unforgettable trek through the woods with Ursula. The forests of Oregon are magical indeed—we discovered an enormous tree stump in the shape of a dragon during our wanderings. Ursula was our guide to this world—she knew the plants and the birds and the huge, moss-covered trees.

Languishing in a suburban desert (literally and metaphorically) in Texas some years later, I had collected a few rejections, which, however personal and nicely worded, were still rejections. I was in a difficult personal situation, exiled from academia for almost a decade, and my family was thousands of miles away in India; my only joys were my daughter and writing. Perhaps it was time to give up writing for the world, and simply scribble for myself. In the midst of this crisis I gathered up my courage and wrote to Ursula. We had already exchanged a few letters by then. I mentioned that I didn't think I had it in me to be a writer—you know, the kind who writes for everyone, not just herself. Ursula asked me to send her a sample of my latest. So I did.

It was her crucial encouragement at this low point in my life that led to my first short story publication, followed by a children's book that came out first in India and then the US (for which Ursula wrote a blurb) and ultimately a steady trickle of science fiction and fantasy short stories. Every once in a while Ursula would ask to read my latest publication and send back comments and congratulations. For a great doyen of the field to take notice of an obscure Indian wannabe writer in the vast sea of America was no small thing for the writer in question. Her loyalty to her craft was such that any praise given was praise earned, and her advice was always sound and to the point. I learned from her, for example, the importance of reading one's work aloud, and how that enables one to become sensitive to the sound of language, to the rhythm and flow of sentences. Her fine book on the tools of writing, *Steering the Craft*, is one I still recommend to new writers.

Over the years my correspondence with Ursula shifted from paper to emails, Our exchanges, though infrequent, were always interesting. We talked about writing, but also about our mutual interest in nonhuman others. We talked at length about climate change (my academic work having moved to that area), the significance of the term Anthropocene (she had been invited to a conference on the subject by Donna Haraway), the meaning of happiness. We discussed the tendency of modern humans to succumb to the techno-fix, even for complex issues like climate change. I think it was clearer to her than to most people that technology by itself can never solve anything (it is more likely to create new problems) if the underlying paradigm remains unchanged. But also, modern technology can be a distraction and an addiction; that we have a lot to learn from Indigenous peoples, and from other species, is apparent in her work, from essays to fiction. Probably one of her most underrated stories is one called "A Man of the People" in the collection *Five Ways to Forgiveness*. Set on the world of Hain, which has the longest history and the greatest technological sophistication of any world in the galaxy of her imagination, it brings to life a pueblo culture that one might call low-tech despite the availability of high-tech. To me this illustrates the possibility of technology arising from and serving the needs and values of the culture, rather than the other way around. We are so familiar with modern technology as the instrument of power, changing and arranging our lives without our participation and consent, that we can't imagine what it would be like to *not* live this way. Ursula saw earlier than others the kinds of dangers that behemoths like Amazon and Google pose to the world—the arrival of the corpocracy and the undermining of democracy and the artistic imagination. Her fiery speech at the National Book Awards ceremony in 2014 is testimony to that. They must still be beating out the flames from the walls. "We live in capitalism. Its power seems inescapable. So did the divine right of kings. Any human power can be resisted and changed by human beings. Resistance and change often begin in art, and very often in our art, the art of words."

As Timmi DuChamp notes in her tribute, Ursula Le Guin possessed a quality that places her among the greatest of writers and seers—a moral imagination.

I got to see Ursula for the third and last time in January 2014. I had gone up to Portland for an academic conference, and Molly and Ursula and I had lunch at a nice restaurant. We talked about everything in the universe and more. Later, we took pictures with my camera, but there was something wrong with it, so only one of the pictures materialized, a lovely one of Ursula and Molly. I remember us standing at the edge of the street in Portland. There was snow in the cracks on the sidewalk, a row of cars parallel parked, and the bare-armed trees lining the narrow road. We were laughing in the afternoon light, saying goodbye, and the snow-topped visage of Mt. Hood was somewhere in the sky, although I can't remember if it was visible from that particular street at that moment.

When, in 2015, the Science Fiction Research Association invited me to be one of their three keynote speakers, I chose to speak about the relevance of one of Ursula's most famous short stories, "The Ones Who Walk Away from Omelas." I had a certain interpretation of it in the light of what I'd learned about climate change and the history of science, and I was nervous about revealing half-baked ideas before a bunch of literary scholars. I also wanted to end my talk with a wolf howl. So I emailed Ursula and aired my thoughts, which she validated and complicated for me. "Howl if you feel like it!" she wrote. She told me she had hooted like a great horned owl in the Library of Congress. So, of course, I did.

The last time I heard from Ursula, last year, she hadn't been very well. She said that she would not always be able to respond to my emails but they were still welcome. During the year I sent a couple of missives. Then, on January 23, 2018, I heard the news of her passing the previous day.

In the *Earthsea* series, there are two great ruminations on death. *The Farthest Shore* is the first one, and the last book, *The Other Wind*, is the second. In *The Farthest Shore*, Cob, an old mage who fears death, has made himself immortal, but only at the cost of life itself and the balance of the world. The hero Ged makes a great journey across the seas and islands of Earthsea, seeking the place from which to restore the balance. Eventually he and his companion find themselves in land of death, "the dry land," separated from the place of the living by a stone wall, where the stars never move and lovers pass each other like strangers in the streets. Here they find Cob, who declares that his body will not decay and die. Ged says to him: "A living body suffers pain, Cob; a living body grows old; it dies. Death is the price we pay for our life and for all life. . . . You sold the green earth and the sun and stars to save yourself."

The struggle that ensues is not the stuff of sword and sorcery but a struggle to overcome fear, to be complete in the world, to be free. By freeing Cob, at great cost to himself, Ged restores the balance of the world.

To me this is one of the finest illustrations of the power and relevance of imaginative literature. Consider our present world—the madness of the potentates, the corporate coup d'état of nations worldwide, the taking apart of the planetary systems that sustain life on Earth. I wonder if behind all the machinations of the super-rich and the escapes and addictions and imperatives of modern industrial civilization—if behind all these phenomena lies a pathological fear of death, and of suffering. Death and suffering are fearsome indeed, but would you sell the green earth and the sun and the stars to be free of them?

In the last book of *Earthsea*, Le Guin returns to the land of death to unbuild the last wall. By the end of the book, the dead, condemned for so long to walk in a pale imitation of life endlessly through the streets of the dry land, are set free. They are free to be sunlight and leaves and water, to return to the great cycle, the dance of the cosmos.

I'm turning the pages of *The Other Wind*, trying to find the quote I am remembering, because my words fall short of what I want to say. In Tehanu's words, then, near the end of the book: "When I die, I can breathe back the breath that made me live. I can give back to the world all that I didn't do. All that I might have been and couldn't be. . . . To the lives that haven't been lived yet. That will be my gift back to the world that gave me the life I did live, the love I loved, the breath I breathed."

Thank you, Ursula Aunty (as you used to sign your emails to me) for your gift to the world and to me. I will look for you in the sunlight and the wind, and in the faces of people at the next great uprising. See you on the Overfell, in Earthsea.

Bibliography

Chapbooks

Distances. Novella. Seattle: Aqueduct Press, 2008.

Of Love and Other Monsters. Seattle: Aqueduct Press, 2005.

Collections

Ambiguity Machines and Other Stories. Northampton, MA: Small Beer Press, 2018. New Delhi: Zubaan, 2018.

Breaking the Bow: Stories Inspired by the Ramayana. Edited by Vandana Singh and Anil Menon. New Delhi: Zubaan, 2012.

The Woman Who Thought She Was a Planet and Other Stories. New Delhi: Zubaan/Penguin India, 2009.

Children's and YA Fiction

"Almaru." *Shockwave! and Other Cyber Stories.* New Delhi: Penguin Books India, 2007.

"A Martian Homecoming." *7 Science Fiction Stories.* New York: Scholastic India, 2006.

Younguncle in the Himalayas. New Delhi: Zubaan, 2005.

Younguncle Comes to Town. New Delhi: Zubaan, 2004; New York: Viking Children's Books, 2006.

Short Stories

"Sticky Man." *Lady Churchill's Rosebud Wristlet* (*LCRW*) no. 42, November 2020. Edited by Gavin Grant and Kelly Link. Northampton, MA: Small Beer Press, 2020.

"Mother Ocean." *Current Futures: A Sci-Fi Ocean Anthology.* X Prize. June 2019. https://go.xprize.org/oceanstories/.

"Reunion." *The Gollancz Book of South Asian Science Fiction Vol. 1.* Edited by Tarun K. Saint. Gurugram, India: Hachette India, 2019.

"Requiem." *Ambiguity Machines and Other Stories.*" Northampton, MA: Small Beer Press, 2018; New Delhi: Zubaan, 2018.

"Widdam." *The Magazine of Fantasy and Science Fiction.* January/February 2018. https://www.sfsite.com/fsf/toc1801.htm.

"The Mountain." *Mithila Review* no. 9. India: September 2017.

"Shikasta." *Visions, Ventures, Escape Velocities.* Edited by Ed Finn and Joey Eschrich. The Center for Science and Imagination, ASU-NASA, Tempe, AZ. December 2017. https://csi.asu.edu/books/vvev/.

"Of Wind and Fire." *To Shape the Dark.* Edited by Athena Andreadis. Cambridge, MA: Candlemark and Gleam, May 2016. http://www.candlemarkandgleam.com/shop/to-shape-the-dark/.

"Ambiguity Machines: An Examination." April 2015. http://www.tor.com/stories/2015/04/ambiguity-machines-an-examination-vandana-singh.

"Arctic Light." *Eat the Sky, Drink the Ocean.* Edited by Kirsty Murray, Payal Dhar, and Anita Roy. Delhi: Zubaan, 2014/London: Allen and Unwin, 2015.

"Entanglement." Originally published online by the Hieroglyph
    Project, 2014. https://hieroglyph.asu.edu/story/entanglement/.

"Wake-Rider." *Lightspeed Magazine* no. 55. Adamant Press, December
    2014. https://www.lightspeedmagazine.com/fiction/wake-rider/.

"Cry of the Kharchal." *Clarkesworld* no. 83, August 2013. http://
    clarkesworldmagazine.com/prior/issue_83/.

"Peripateia." *The End of the Road: An Anthology of Original Fiction.*
    Edited by Jonathan Oliver. New York: Solaris, 2013.

"Sailing the Antarsa." *The Other Half of the Sky.* Edited by Athena
    Andreadis and Kay T. Holt. Cambridge, MA: Candlemark and
    Gleam, 2013.

"With Fate Conspire." *Solaris Rising 2: The New Solaris Book of Science
    Fiction.* Edited by Ian Whates. New York and Oxford: Solaris,
    2013.

"A Handful of Rice." *Steampunk III: Steampunk Revolution.* Edited by
    Ann VanderMeer. San Francisco: Tachyon Publications, 2012.

"Ruminations in an Alien Tongue." *Lightspeed Magazine* no. 23. Edited
    by John Joseph Adams. Adamant Press, April 2012. https://gizmodo.
    com/lightspeed-presents-ruminations-in-an-alien-tongue-5898416.

"Indra's Web." *TRSF: The Best New Science Fiction.* Edited by Stephen
    Cass. Cambridge, MA: Technology Review, Inc., 2011.

"Are You Sannata3159?" *The Company He Keeps.* Edited by Peter
    Crowther and Nick Gevers. Hornsea, East Yorkshire: PS
    Publishing, 2010.

"Somadeva: A Sky River Sutra." *Strange Horizons,* March 29, 2010.
    http://strangehorizons.com/fiction/somadeva-a-sky-river-sutra.

"Oblivion: A Journey." *Clockwork Phoenix: Tales of Beauty and Strangeness.* Edited by Mike Allen. Los Angeles: Norilana Books, 2008.

"Almaru." *Shockwave! and Other Cyber Stories.* New Delhi: Penguin Books India, 2007.

"Hunger." *Interfictions: An Anthology of Interstitial Writing.* Edited by Delia Sherman and Theodora Goss. Northampton, MA: Interstitial Arts Foundation through Small Beer Press, 2007.

"Life-Pod." *Foundation Issue 100.* Edited by Farah Mendlesohn and Graham Sleight. UK: Science Fiction Foundation, Summer 2007.

"The Sign in the Window." *Rabid Transit: Menagerie.* Edited by Ratbastards. Rabid Transit Press, 2005.

"The Tetrahedron." *InterNova: The Magazine of International Science Fiction: Unexplored Territories* no. 1. Edited by Ronald M. Hahn, Olaf G. Hilscher, and Michael K. Iwoleit. Norderstedt: Books on Demand GmbH, 2005.

"Delhi." *So Long Been Dreaming: Postcolonial Science Fiction.* Edited by Nalo Hopkinson and Uppinder Mehan. Vancouver: Arsenal Pulp Press, 2004.

"Thirst." *The Third Alternative* no. 40. TTA Press, Winter 2004.

"Three Tales from Sky River." *Strange Horizons* no. 5. Edited by Susan Marie Groppi. January 2004. http://strangehorizons.com/fiction/three-tales-from-sky-river-myths-for-a-starfaring-age/.

"The Wife." *Polyphony Volume 3.* Edited by Deborah Layne and Jay Lake. Wilsonville, OR: Wheatland Press, 2003.

"The Woman Who Thought She Was a Planet." *Trampoline.* Edited by Kelly Link. Northampton, MA: Small Beer Press, 2003. Reprinted in *The Woman Who Thought She Was a Planet and Other Stories.* New Delhi: Zubaan/Penguin Books India, 2008.

"The Room on the Roof." *Polyphony Vol. 1.* Edited by Deborah Layne and Jay Lake. Wilsonville, OR: Wheatland Press, 2002.

For a more complete bibliography, including reprints of short stories, visit http://vandana-writes.com.

About the Author

VANDANA SINGH IS A writer of speculative fiction and a professor of physics at a small and lively public university near Boston. Her critically acclaimed short stories have been reprinted in numerous best-of-year anthologies, and her most recent collection, *Ambiguity Machines and Other Stories* (Small Beer Press and Zubaan, 2018) was a finalist for the Philip K. Dick award. A particle physicist by training, she has been working for a decade on a transdisciplinary, justice-based conceptualization of the climate crisis at the nexus of science, pedagogy, and society. She is a Fellow of the Center for Science and the Imagination at Arizona State University. She was born and raised in India, where she continues to have multiple entanglements, both personal and professional, and divides her time between New Delhi and the Boston area. She can be found on the web at http://vandana-writes.com/.

FRIENDS OF

These are indisputably momentous times—the financial system is melting down globally and the Empire is stumbling. Now more than ever there is a vital need for radical ideas.

In the years since its founding—and on a mere shoestring—PM Press has risen to the formidable challenge of publishing and distributing knowledge and entertainment for the struggles ahead. With hundreds of releases to date, we have published an impressive and stimulating array of literature, art, music, politics, and culture. Using every available medium, we've succeeded in connecting those hungry for ideas and information to those putting them into practice.

Friends of PM allows you to directly help impact, amplify, and revitalize the discourse and actions of radical writers, filmmakers, and artists. It provides us with a stable foundation from which we can build upon our early successes and provides a much-needed subsidy for the materials that can't necessarily pay their own way. You can help make that happen—and receive every new title automatically delivered to your door once a month—by joining as a Friend of PM Press. And, we'll throw in a free T-shirt when you sign up.

Here are your options:
- $30 a month: Get all books and pamphlets plus 50% discount on all webstore purchases
- $40 a month: Get all PM Press releases (including CDs and DVDs) plus 50% discount on all webstore purchases
- $100 a month: Superstar—Everything plus PM merchandise, free downloads, and 50% discount on all webstore purchases

For those who can't afford $30 or more a month, we have Sustainer Rates at $15, $10, and $5. Sustainers get a free PM Press T-shirt and a 50% discount on all purchases from our website.

Your Visa or Mastercard will be billed once a month, until you tell us to stop. Or until our efforts succeed in bringing the revolution around. Or the financial meltdown of Capital makes plastic redundant. Whichever comes first.

PM Press is an independent, radical publisher of books and media to educate, entertain, and inspire. Founded in 2007 by a small group of people with decades of publishing, media, and organizing experience, PM Press amplifies the voices of radical authors, artists, and activists. Our aim is to deliver bold political ideas and vital stories to all walks of life and arm the dreamers to demand the impossible. We have sold millions of copies of our books, most often one at a time, face to face. We're old enough to know what we're doing and young enough to know what's at stake. Join us to create a better world.

PM Press
PO Box 23912
Oakland, CA 94623
510-658-3906 • info@pmpress.org

PM Press in Europe
europe@pmpress.org
www.pmpress.org.uk

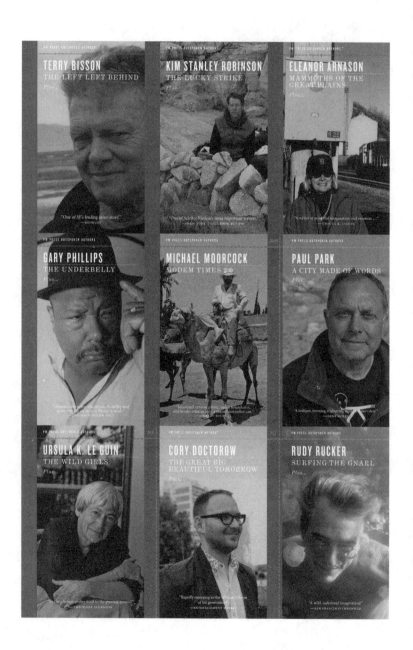

PM PRESS OUTSPOKEN AUTHORS

TERRY BISSON
THE LEFT LEFT BEHIND
Plus…

"One of SF's leading innovators."
—BOOKLIST

PM PRESS OUTSPOKEN AUTHORS

KIM STANLEY ROBINSON
THE LUCKY STRIKE
Plus…

"One of Science Fiction's most important writers."
—NEW YORK TIMES BOOK REVIEW

PM PRESS OUTSPOKEN AUTHORS

ELEANOR ARNASON
MAMMOTHS OF THE GREAT PLAINS
Plus…

"A writer of powerful imagination and creation…"
—URSULA K. LE GUIN

PM PRESS OUTSPOKEN AUTHORS

GARY PHILLIPS
THE UNDERBELLY
Plus…

"Intensely… with a robust, diabolical and good-natured glee."
—THE WASHINGTON POST

PM PRESS OUTSPOKEN AUTHORS

MICHAEL MOORCOCK
MODEM TIMES 2.0

"Moorcock crosses genres, bends boundaries, and breaks rules as only a master storyteller can."
—LIBRARY JOURNAL

PM PRESS OUTSPOKEN AUTHORS

PAUL PARK
A CITY MADE OF WORDS
Plus…

"A brilliant, stunning, frightening tour de force."
—GENE WOLFE

PM PRESS OUTSPOKEN AUTHORS

URSULA K. LE GUIN
THE WILD GIRLS
Plus…

"Le Guin brings us a story to rival the growing ground."
—CHRISTOPHER ISHERWOOD

PM PRESS OUTSPOKEN AUTHORS

CORY DOCTOROW
THE GREAT BIG BEAUTIFUL TOMORROW
Plus…

"Rapidly emerging as the William Gibson of his generation."
—ENTERTAINMENT WEEKLY

PM PRESS OUTSPOKEN AUTHORS

RUDY RUCKER
SURFING THE GNARL
Plus…

"A wild, undextered imagination!"
—SAN FRANCISCO CHRONICLE